ROUGH PASSAGES

K. M. HERKES

DAWNRIGGER
Publishing

Print ISBN: 978-1-945745-13-3

Electronic ISBN: 978-1-945745-12-6

Cover artwork and design by Quincy J. Allen

Published by Dawnrigger Publishing

dawnrigger.com

Printed in the USA

WHAT PEOPLE ARE SAYING ABOUT
ROUGH PASSAGES

It is certainly a book from cover to cover.

SATISFIED BUYER

Pages and pages of words!

THAT GUY WHO'S ALWAYS AT THE COFFEE SHOP

Too much swearing.

SOMEONE TOTALLY NOT RELATED TO THE
AUTHOR

ROUGH PASSAGES

Paul, without you, I would still be only a dreamer of daydreams, not a published author.
Your steadfast support and encouragement make my creative adventures possible. No dedication, no acknowledgement, no words will ever be sufficient to express my gratitude and love.
This will have to do.

To my faithful alpha & beta readers: your patience, enthusiasm, and generosity continue to amaze and humble me. Your critical observations, pivotal insights, and meticulous attention to detail are essential to polishing my lumpy ideas into shining stories.
Thank you all.

This one's for you, Dan'l. I finally did it.
Guess I'll let you get back to what you were doing.
I miss you something fierce.

EXTRAORDINARY

PART 1: A SPECIAL DAY

VALERIE LOVED THE CARNIVAL. Every April, it set up in the Indio city park for one magic week, and every year, she celebrated her birthday there. The year she turned forty-two, she got to watch everything come to life while she ran all her unpleasant annual errands. Having the day free from both jobs felt like a holiday even if she spent it on obligations.

Partially-constructed machinery rose against the sunlit Santa Rosa Mountains like dinosaur skeletons as she drove to the DMV. The rides were running by the time she passed on the way back. Their colored lights flashed pale under the bright blue sky, and she caught tinny scraps of familiar melodies on the hot breeze through her open window. Piles of canvas and wood became a colorful lane of gaming booths and exhibits between her trip to the gynecologist and the one to the Public Safety Clinic where she took her R-factor test.

On impulse she pulled over to the curb to watch two of the crew lift a sign into place. *Cotton Candy*! it proclaimed in a rainbow of pastels, and the cook maneuvering her machine into position shouted curses at them when the panel smacked her in passing. Valerie took a deep breath of air heavy with the residue of gasoline fumes and the salty-sweet promise of caramel popcorn before she reluctantly drove on.

Anticipating the coming evening kept her so preoccupied that she barely felt the usual twinge of nervousness as her blood was drawn. While she waited in the chilly exam room for the usual post-test medical lecture she read posters about cancerous moles and the warning signs of heart attacks and reflected that getting older was dangerous for everyone. Only one in every few thousand came up positive for rollover these days. Valerie wiped her hands dry and reminded herself that she was far more likely to get cancer than end up turning into a monster.

The clinic nurse delivered the usual warnings about watching her weight and wearing sunscreen. She made it sound like Valerie had chosen to be born pasty-pale and prone to putting on pounds despite being on her feet all day. Her ankles were swollen, she noticed. The buzzing fluorescent lights made her blonde hair look green in the door mirror. The roots were showing, and her bangs needed a trim.

The nurse also wanted Valerie to make another appointment to go over the blood test results with a doctor. Valerie signed the release forms to get a letter instead, and she hurried to her car to get the rest of her errands finished. One nagging session a year was enough.

She didn't have time for another lecture about preparing for the worst and planning for her family's future anyway. She'd used up all her favors to get these few hours free for herself. Usually day shifts at the diner and night hours at another restaurant kept her life full, and shuttling her mother to and from physical therapy filled the gaps.

Besides, she'd heard the be-prepared speech twice already, at forty and forty-one. The warnings were all pointless. If she was unlucky enough to roll, then Public Safety would come to her, the way they'd taken away a customer from her night job a few months earlier. The poor man's friends abandoned him at the fancy restaurant table when everything started icing over, while he sat there looking terrified as things frosted over white and crumbled all around him. He'd cried when the retrieval team took him away.

Valerie turned up the car stereo to drown out the memory of those whimpers. She didn't have time to worry about things that wouldn't happen. She still had to buy groceries for the week and drop off bills at the post office before she could pick up her mother and the boys and go have fun.

By the time she got her family to the carnival the sun was down, and the line for tickets stretched down the block. Not even the long wait with her cranky mother and two rambunctious toddlers could dampen her spirits.

Sweat made her sundress stick to her breasts and thighs, she got wood chips in her sandals, and they stood near a rancid garbage can far too long, but the raucous laughter from people swooping past on the roller coaster took her back to times when happiness was a matter of giving herself a stomach ache from too much popcorn and taking too many spins on the teacup ride.

Her sons, Gary and Johnny, caught her infectious enthusiasm and spent long minutes deciding which concession stands to visit, and then they had a serious discussion on the relative merits of neon-braided lollipops and purple puffs of cotton candy. The proprietors smiled at their thoughtful scowls and their matching blue shorts outfits.

They were in a phase when their clothes fit, and they had a rosy-cheeked blond beauty that invited indulgence. Sometimes she saw their father's calculating selfishness in their smiles and his obsessive anger in their frowning squabbles, but moments like these were ones she wished would last forever.

The moment didn't last. Of course it didn't.

Cotton candy won the snack war, but Gary fell headlong on the path of wood chips between the concession area and the aisles of gaming booths before he took a single bite. He scraped both his knees and ruined his new jeans, and while Valerie was distracted by his tears and the cleanup, Johnny ate his all of his little brother's cotton candy as well as his own. Five minutes after that, Valerie was holding Johnny over a trash barrel while he vomited it all back up.

Valerie wiped his face and gave him a sip of her icy drink, trying hard to ignore the fact that her clothes were now sopping wet with tears, snot and spatters of vomit. Then she embraced Johnny and glared at her mother over his shoulder. "You could've told me he was stuffing it all down his throat."

Mom leaned on her walker and sniffed in disapproval. "The greedy little pig learned his lesson. He'll thank you for it later. You're too soft on them."

Valerie held her breath so that she would not say, "And maybe if you'd been a little softer with me, I wouldn't be raising two boys alone while I work two jobs to pay off debts run up by my abusive addict ex-husband." If Mom heard all that she would cry, and when she cried everyone blamed Valerie.

Mom looked like the big, soft, apple-cheeked grandma she

pretended to be. She hid her flinty cold heart beneath an ample bosom and wrapped herself in flowery house dresses, and she kept all the hard bitterness inside. There was no point in arguing, so all Valerie said was, "Mom, please. Not tonight."

Then she looked around at the hustle and bustle and blinked back tears. Barkers shouted, music played, and people strolled past on all sides, politely ignoring the family tension in their midst. Tent walls swayed in the cool breeze, the air was dusty and thick with grease, and flashing rides spun and rattled like monsters moving in the twilight.

It was perfect, except that her heart was full of acid sadness, and she ached for all the years she'd wasted trying to be a good child and then a good wife instead of a real person. For all she knew, she'd wasted her whole life. If her R-test came back positive, this might be her last proper carnival ever, at least as a free woman.

She shoved the morbid thought away. Rollover wasn't a death sentence. Not these days. Most factor-positive people led full, normal lives even after the changes. And they tipped well. Other servers would whisper "Poz" to each other and pretend they were too busy to serve rollovers, but Valerie was happy to take the tables and the tips.

But it wasn't going to happen to her.

A hawker for one of the game booths leaned over his counter and waved, catching her eye. "How about a free game for the kiddos?" he called out. A gold tooth flashed in his scruffy beard, and he tipped the velvet top hat on his shaggy dark hair. "And one for their beautiful mother."

Mom snorted. "Beautiful? You? He must be blind."

The insult poked right through Valerie's temper and let the all sourness drain out.

"Well, Mom," she said, "people do say I look just like you."

They had looked alike once, before age hunched Mom's spine and shriveled her skin, before the accident broke her hip and bed rest added even more padding to her soft body. They were both big women with thick arms and thicker ankles, and the color in their hair came from the same bottles these days. Valerie smirked at her mother's shocked expression and took her sons by the hand. "Come on, guys. This will be fun."

The boys walked fast and bouncy. The words *free* and *fun* were enough to make them forget the earlier small tragedies, and they left Mom, her poisonous tongue and her walker far behind. Valerie didn't care if the woman ever caught up, but of course she did. The nasty comment went unremarked. Things ignored ceased to exist. That was Mom's way. They spent a lot of evenings not speaking to each other.

The boys tossed balls at painted boats floating in tubs of moving water, and Valerie chatted with the man running the game. He had a polished patter and a rough, gritty charm. The boys cheered, water splashed, and Valerie paid for two more games after the first and considered it a fair bargain. The harmless flirting made her feel alive again.

"Bah," Mom said. "Will you look at that? Back in my day, the freaks stayed in the sideshow tents. Disgusting."

The boys both turned, blue eyes gleaming with curiosity, and Valerie turned too. Her stomach knotted up. She already knew from Mom's words what would be there.

Visitors flashing bare skin and dressed in gaudy colors filled the path going both directions. The two women in gray and black Department of Public Safety uniforms walking away along the other side stood out for reasons beyond their drab wardrobes. They were visibly R-positive rollovers, and they walked in a bubble of space, untouched by the jostling crowds.

Both were tall and fit, and one of them looked normal except for the purple hair she kept in a thick braid. The length of it should have dangled past her waist, but instead it writhed and twisted like a live creature. She walked with both hands around it to keep it from questing towards people. The other officer had cropped short black hair, a scaled gray muzzle of a face, spiny lumps where most people had ears, and—

Gary crowed with laughter and shouted, "Look, Mama, he's all scaly."

"And a tail!" Johnny said even louder. "He has a tail coming out of his pants. I want a tail, Mommy!"

Valerie's heart started to beat fast, and she said the first thing that came to mind. "She, sweeties. *She* has scales. Hush, please. Use your Sunday voices."

"I WANT A TAIL," Johnny bellowed.

The DPS officers stopped to look, and Valerie sincerely wished the ground would open up and swallow her whole. The pair exchanged a glance and changed direction. The one who looked like a scaly gray lizard swung her tail wide as she walked, the one with the purple braid let it wander free, and the crowd gave them an even wider berth.

As they approached, Gary hid behind Valerie's legs the way he always did when people got too close, but Johnny tugged at her hand. "Tail, Mom. TAIL!"

"I'm so sorry," Valerie said to the women, then hefted up her indignant older boy-child before he could lunge at them. "Johnny, tell the nice ladies you're sorry for being rude."

"No," he shouted in Valerie's ear, and then he wrapped his

arms around her neck so he could sniffle into her collar. "Not sorry! Wanna tail, mama."

"Just like his father," Mom said under her breath. "Want-want-want. Well. At least he knows you don't apologize to animals. Honestly, Valerie, I raised you better than this."

She looked the two women up and down in a breathtaking display of bad manners, and then she curled her lip and hobbled away. Her walker made emphatic little crunches as she scooted it along.

"Honestly," Valerie said to no one in particular, "no, she didn't. I apologize."

The purple-haired woman had friendly eyes and generous lips that parted in a broad grin over straight white teeth. "No need. You weren't the rude one. And don't worry on our account. We've heard far worse at public outreach meetings. We don't mind showing off for your kid there, if you don't mind. Children are naturally curious. Teaching acceptance and tolerance early pays off."

Sympathy and kindness were the hardest reactions to absorb without breaking down. The only reason Valerie didn't burst into tears on the spot was that she *couldn't*. Not in front of the boys. Her eyes stung, and she slid Johnny off her hip to the ground. "Thank you."

She held both Johnny's hands tight just in case he still had ideas about grabbing anyone's tail, and he announced, "I'm not saying sorry because I'm not, and I don't lie. I want a tail. It isn't fair. Why do you get a tail and I don't?"

The scaly woman said, "If you ever find out the answer to that question, you'll be rich and famous. I can't give you mine, but you can touch it if you want. Want to?"

He nodded, and she twitched her tail around to wrap the tip around his right wrist. The scales glittered, reflecting the fairy lights overhead. Johnny gasped in excitement, and Valerie let go of his hands, saying, "Gently, sweetie, like with the cat."

A second later, she wanted to swallow her tongue, but the woman only laughed, and Johnny said reverently, "It's soft. And warm. I thought it would be cold. We petted a snake at day school."

"Nope. I'm not like a snake. I only get cold in the winter." Fangs showed at the corners of the woman's lipless smile, and her voice lisped slightly. "And the scales flake off one at a time, not like snakeskin. Go ahead, you can tug harder. It won't break."

She sounded so patient. Valerie couldn't imagine letting people poke at her like she was some kind of exhibit, but Johnny was eating it up. Meanwhile, Gary squeezed both arms around her leg. "Go, mommy," he whispered. "Go, now?"

"It's okay, honey." Valerie crouched so she could put her arms around him and kissed him behind his ear. He smelled like baby powder and sugar and little-boy sweat, and his skin felt damp. She weighed the merits of pushing him to be sociable against the likelihood of an emotional meltdown and decided against it.

He scrunched up his shoulders and buried his face against her neck.

"He's shy around strangers," she said, needing to say something. "Sorry."

"Maybe we shouldn't be strangers then." The purple-haired woman went down on one knee and smiled at Gary's back. "Hey, little guy. I'm Gwen. That's Miss Jen over there."

Johnny said, "This is totally flair, Gary. I'm touching it, see?"

Gary turned his head to see his brother and stuffed most of his fist in his mouth.

"Look at those big baby blues," Gwen said. The tip of her braid appeared at the top of her shoulder as if it wanted a look of its own. "I bet your mama has a hard time saying no to those eyes. I know I would."

The boy looked up at Valerie then. Pale blue eyes ran in her family, and his were adorable, even red-rimmed and puffy from crying. She winked at him because that always made him giggle. Her eyes had been the same color as his, but they were going green as she got older. A few weeks ago, one of the chefs had asked if she'd gotten contact lenses. Gary grinned around his knuckle and waved his other hand at Gwen. "Hurrgh."

Gwen said, "Is that so?"

"He likes your hair." Valerie held out a hand to Gwen. "Valerie Wade. It's nice to meet you. This is Gary."

The DPS officer smiled and accepted the handshake, and Gary said, "Gahmah!"

Then he waved his gooey fingers at Gwen. His gaze was still fixed on her braid, which had snuck over her shoulder to hang down the front. She shook one of his fingers, gently. "Very nice to meet you too. Are you a fan of purple?"

"Gah!" he said emphatically. Harold and the Purple Crayon was his favorite bedtime story.

"I like purple too," Gwen said, "but my hair isn't for playing, sorry. Not like Jen's tail. You can wave to it, though. It'll wave back. Say hello, hair."

The braid flicked up and down, then disappeared behind her back. Gary's lip quivered, but he mumbled, "Gamahah," and let Johnny help him pet Gwen's tail instead of getting stubborn.

Jen had a quick-pics camera and took photos for them, patiently answering questions until the boys' attention began to wander. Jen disengaged from their clinging hands with an ease that spoke of long practice working with children, while Gwen distracted them by using loosened strands of hair to remove two carnival tokens from a shirt pocket and offered them up.

"Would you boys like tokens for the games?" she asked. The Department gives them out as prizes for children who are polite and brave, and I think you qualify."

That was a lie. The DPS didn't give out money. Valerie swallowed the prideful protest that she didn't need charity. It wasn't for her, after all. Johnny and Gary each took a token, and Johnny gave Jen a smile as bright as the sun and said thank you with only a little prompting.

The two officers sauntered off into the crowd, and Valerie took the boys down the midway to let them pick a place to lose their money. When they held a whispered conversation that ended up with two dollars going to a charity dunk tank *because good works, Mama,* her heart nearly burst with pride.

Her mother rejoined her while the boys were pitching softballs with the help of the proprietor, whose dripping wet partner was not pleased about them getting assistance.

Mom didn't say anything, of course. Valerie heard the rattle of the walker and imagined her standing a few feet away, frowning until her eyes disappeared in wrinkles.

"Hi, Mom," Valerie said in her best chipper customer-service voice. "Isn't this fun?"

"You always did love the carnival," Mom said, and then she sighed. "I didn't mean to ruin it tonight. I hope I didn't. I just don't know why the poz can't keep themselves to themselves. It scares me, what the world's coming to. You can't always tell by looking at them, you know. Look at that woman who burned down Boston last summer. She could've been anyone, but she was a monster. They ought to wear signs or something."

"Boise, Mom. It was Boise, and—never mind." It was impossible to stay angry. Mom was old, and in pain, and nothing was going to change her mind. When Valerie turned around, she saw sadness and regrets. She made herself smile. "Let's try and have one good evening together. Please?"

Mom said, "I did my best, you know. It wasn't easy, raising three of you on my own after your dad left. I didn't want you to make my mistakes, that's all."

"I know, Mom. You did your best."

It hadn't been easy on any of them. That was why Mom's other two daughters no longer spoke to her. Valerie didn't blame Mom for her own mistakes. She'd listened to everyone who told her how she should behave, she'd trusted teachers who told her she was stupid, and she'd believed her husband when he said he loved her.

Almost a year ago now, she'd looked at John's sorrowing face while the imprint of his hand still stung her cheek, and she'd seen him for what he was. Power and possession were all that mattered. His children's college funds were his to spend on drugs. The rent was his to spend the same way. Valerie was his. He loved the fear his hard fists and harder words caused, but he didn't love her. He never had.

She'd vomited into the sink, grabbed the boys and left the house without looking back. Until that moment, she'd stayed with him because she didn't want to become her mother, but there'd been a worse fate waiting for her in John's hatred.

Putting that mistake behind her took three months, two police calls, all her savings and a restraining order. They would probably be living on the streets if Mom hadn't needed home care and invited them into her tiny apartment.

Valerie couldn't blame Mom for any of it, so she said, "I'm doing my best too. We both are. Truce?"

Mom nodded, appeased, and they did have a good evening, checking out the sights, letting the boys try out the toddler-friendly rides, resting on park benches and letting the world pass by. One diaper change, two minor tantrums, and a dozen mean-spirited Mom comments about the decline of civilization later, Valerie bundled everyone into the car and headed home. It hadn't been the best birthday ever, but it was one she could put in the plus column.

Her happiness crumbled away when she spotted Gwen and Miss Jen waiting near the front door of her apartment building. They sat on one of the courtyard benches under a spreading live oak, and their dark uniforms blended into the shadows cast by the security lights four floors up. If not for the faint glow shimmering around them, she never would've known they were there. Her stomach lurched with fear, wondering why they had come here, and she stopped dead.

The DPS officers got up. Gwen's long purple hair was all loose now, a cloak that swirled around her shoulders even though the cool night air was still. Valerie could see now that it wasn't really hair, more like strands of seaweed or vines. Jen's tail twitched, and her thin lips lifted off the fangs. It didn't look like a smile, and she seemed entirely alien with her deep-set eyes and skin glittering as she emerged from beneath the tree.

"Hi!" Johnny's greeting bounced off the building, but he went from shout to whisper without prompting. "I didn't know the tail and hair ladies lived here too."

His whisper wasn't much softer than his shout, and Gwen

replied, "Sorry, kiddo, we're only visiting." Her hair rippled in time with her words. "We stopped by because we forgot to tell your mom something earlier. Ms. Wade, can we have a moment of your time?"

Mom made a disgusted noise with her tongue and teeth, the sound she usually reserved for one of Gary's potty accidents. "See what happens when you encourage them?" she said. "Now they're following you home."

"They aren't stray puppies, Mom." Valerie hoped the thumping of her heart wasn't audible to anyone else. Fear made her pulse jump and skitter worse than when she had to serve tables full of college boys. "Please take the boys inside."

She said, "Give me a minute," to the DPS officers and got out the apartment key for Mom after she unlocked the building door for them. "Go inside with Nana," she told Johnny as she put Gary's hand into his, and she pushed open the heavy outer door. "I need to talk to the ladies. Be good boys, please?"

Johnny heaved a martyred sigh and tugged Gary inside. Once Mom was through the door, breathing hard and thumping her walker down with every step, the boys bolted ahead towards the elevator, yelling and laughing at the top of their lungs as they went.

Valerie winced. She would be getting a lecture about violating quiet hours from the building supervisor in the morning.

Or maybe she wouldn't.

She walked over to the DPS officers, who both nodded to her but stayed silent.

Valerie said, "My mother thinks you're stalking me."

"No, this is official business," Gwen said. "We were off

duty when we went to the fair, but we're back on the job now. We need to talk. Do you want to sit down?"

"No. Just tell me what's going on. You're scaring me." Valerie suppressed a quiver of terror. "Was my test positive? Am I about to go into rollover?"

The women glanced at each other much the same way they had earlier at the carnival. "Did you get tested recently?" Gwen asked. "That figures. No, we're here because of what you said at the carnival. We didn't realize the significance until later, but once we did, we used one of the quick-pics Jen kept to find you in the national database. And once we reported that, the boss sent us right over."

"What did I say? Was it the cat petting comment? I said I was sorry, didn't I?" Valerie clenched her fists, relaxed them. The fear pooled in her belly, leaving her nauseous. A lifetime of Mom's warnings came crowding into her mind as she backed away. "You can't intern me over an accidental insult. If you try to touch me I'll scream."

Gwen said, "Wait, wait, don't panic."

She and Jen both raised their hands, and Jen added, "We're worried about you—worried on your behalf, I mean. We only want to help."

It would've been more reassuring if Jen hadn't had claws to go along with her scales and teeth, but they both looked so concerned that Valerie held her breath instead of screaming right away. And Jen said, "We mean you no harm, I swear. Please don't be frightened. This is official business, though, and we need to ask some questions. Please. May I?"

Valerie's pulse slowed, and she nodded.

"First, how could you tell I'm a woman?" Jen asked.

"Are you kidding me? That's why you're here scaring me half to death?" The questions poured out of Valerie in a relieved flood. "It's obvious to anyone who can see past a crewcut and trousers. And how is that anyone's business? What kind of person abuses DPS authority over their insecurity?"

Once her emotional outburst dribbled away to silence, Gwen said, "She looks like a big lizard, Ms. Wade. Her rollover left zero reliable visuals, and her physique is well outside human female averages. Even when people know her name and pronouns, it isn't *obvious*. Let me ask you the second question: am I glowing? Is Jen? We are, aren't we?"

They were. It was obvious. Anyone could see it.

Valerie's stomach rolled over again. Maybe not everyone could. "What would it mean if I saw a glow?"

"It means you're in rollover now, or already through it." Gwen's voice was soft with sympathy. "I'm sorry, but that settles it. Only people who've come into their own power can see those auras."

"But I'm not—" Not ready. Not strong enough. Not prepared. "No, it's impossible. I can't be. Look at me. I'm still normal. I don't feel a thing."

"Good," Jen said firmly. "That means you probably won't have any complications, not if you're already far enough along to see our power signatures. Physical variances aren't all that common. Carnies like me and Jen, we're the unlucky ones. You're coming over slow and cool. Best you could ask for, really."

Gwen added, "My educated guess says you'll code as N or B. Do you know what that means? Do you remember the common series designations and variances?"

Valerie remembered. Most of her high school friends had forgotten the information as soon as they passed their Health finals, but she'd studied the charts obsessively. When she was fourteen and her first test came up positive, she daydreamed about hitting rollover early and having a tragic death that would make everyone appreciate what they'd lost.

Every fever had been early onset as a pyro, every rash and cramp a sign that she was about to roll as a plague-carrier. She got over it when she passed the high end of the early onset age range, but the facts stuck. The N-series all had some affinity for living matter, while B's were sensory and detection talents.

Both series shared one critical advantage, as far as Valerie was concerned. "N's and B's don't have to be interned, right? I wouldn't have to leave home?"

"Correct—if I'm right. I'm not a diagnostics specialist. We're going to have to ask you to come back to the offices with us to get tested and registered. Will you come voluntarily?"

"Now?" Valerie couldn't help herself. She looked up, towards the lit window of her apartment. Mom would be nagging them through the nightly tooth-brushing and pajama rituals, unless she'd already fallen asleep on the couch. "Right now? Can it wait? I could come tomorrow before work."

Her brain started spinning through possibilities. She would have to get up at 4 AM to make it work with her schedule. She was on breakfast shift at the diner. What if she was interned after all? What if she couldn't come back? The boys needed more stability and guidance than their grandmother could give them. Their father was unreliable when he wasn't being abusive. They needed their mother. They needed her.

Every cell in her body yearned to be with them now.

What would happen to them if she had to be interned?

Gwen and Jen moved back and apart, bracketing her, and

Gwen said, "Sure, it can wait until morning, if you don't mind putting your kids at risk. Like I said, I'm not an expert. Extrasensory variances are common in all the elemental series. If you do flare hot all of a sudden, or turn carnie in front of them, or draw all the air out of their bodies..."

That was a low blow but a fair one. Tears stung Valerie's eyes. She could not put her babies at risk. "No, you're right. Of course I'll come with you now. Can I at least say good-night? Just in case?"

Just in case she couldn't come home again.

"Of course. We'll have to come with you," Gwen said, "and you can't—you won't—shouldn't—oh, this is so hard. I hate this part." Her face was tight with sympathy. "I'm so sorry. I have to say it. Don't touch them. Just in case."

"Oh." All the fear and grief burst up and out through Valerie's chest in a cold explosion, and she couldn't hold back the tears any longer. Then the worst hit her like a punch to the heart. "Oh, God. How am I going to break this to Mom? She doesn't even know I'm poz."

She'd plucked her test results out of the mail, that all-important first time, then forged her name onto her older sister's clearance letter and kept the secret forevermore. How could she admit that she was everything her mother hated?

Jen bared her fangs. "Can I tell her for you? It'd be my pleasure."

It wasn't funny. It was mean and petty, but she laughed because Jen's smile was like a warm hug that said, "I under-stand," and "It will all work out," and most importantly, it said, "You won't have to face this alone."

Oh, that last promise made her dizzy, and the tears that welled up were ones of joy. Everything was about to change, but maybe—just maybe—it wouldn't be the disaster she had dreaded all her life. Maybe this was another step on the road to becoming herself.

"No, I can do it," she said, and pride made her straighten up and smile, because it was true. "I can do this.

PART 2: AN ORDINARY LIFE

THE DEAD MAN walked into the diner on a Tuesday. When Valerie turned at the chime of the doorbell, she was carrying two plates and a pot of coffee to the first booth and worrying about the infant crying at the four-top in the corner. She forgot to keep her inner eyes closed.

He looked like a kid, maybe eighteen, thin and tall. His skin was deep brown, his hair buzzed so short his scalp shone through the fuzz. The uniform identified him as a Marine, probably passing through town on liberty from 29 Palms.

More importantly though, he was dead. To Valerie's eyes, his skull glowed through his skin and his spirit shone like fire inside his veins, pulsing with every heartbeat. In a few days, a few weeks at most, that vibrant life force would leave his body. It was as clear as the friendly smile on the boy's face.

Both plates and the coffee pot hit the floor, and it was all she could do to keep her screams inside. Everyone in the place turned to stare. It was 3:30 in the afternoon. The diner was full with shift workers from the packing plants and kids getting after school snacks. The air conditioner sputtered loud in the silence after the crash, bravely attempting to cool off the dusty blast of desert air the dead man had brought inside with him.

Valerie tore her gaze away from him to the disastrous mess at her feet. One of her sneakers was ruined. Hot brown liquid soaked through the bleach-thinned canvas, pooling warm against the plastic sole under her toes. The scent of coffee, strawberry soda and wet fries filled the air, and she swallowed down nausea.

Her DPS mentor had described what impending death might look like when she saw it. He'd even warned her how hard that first vision might hit her, but she'd never expected it to happen at work. Dying people didn't usually walk into roadside diners and order lunch. Except this one had.

The shift workers went back to their burgers and gossip, sunlight slanting golden and hot across the booths. The schoolboys applauded and laughed, and Valerie pulled her cleaning rag from her apron pocket. Her knees popped when she knelt.

The dying Marine edged carefully past the coffee puddle and took a stool at the counter as if he hadn't just ruined Valerie's day. As if he wasn't *dying*.

The swinging door to the kitchen slammed open to the wall, narrowly missing Nancy, who was working the counter. She didn't even flinch. She was big-haired, bleached-blonde, and married to Jeff, the burly-armed bald owner, which meant she was used to ignoring his tantrums. She also ignored the Marine.

Jeff came barreling over with a bus tub in his big hands and a thunderous expression on his sweaty face. The tub landed next to Valerie in the puddle, splashing coffee over her stockings and the other shoe. That was going to smell lovely by end of shift.

She picked up shards of glass and soggy beef patties, and Jeff loomed over her, breathing his nasty stale smoker's breath down her neck and not lifting a finger.

"What is wrong with you, poz?" he asked "That's the fifth

meal you've dropped since you came back to work from paid leave. Waste of time and my tax money. I'm taking this out of your check, you know. Give me one good reason not to fire your ass."

"Because I'll sue your ass for discrimination?"

It was an empty threat, and unfortunately Jeff knew it. Valerie couldn't afford a lawyer or the time a court case would demand. She couldn't even afford to say the magic words, "You can't fire me, I quit."

She could not risk everything on a bold gamble. Not when she had two kids to feed and clothe and a sick mother with too many bills to pay. Not when she'd bet wrong so many times in her life. No, she needed this job, so she wrung out her towel and made her best play to keep it. "And don't forget I've rolled now. Who knows what I might do to you if you make me angry?"

It was a bluff—she was utterly harmless—but by law Jeff couldn't ask for her case details. She planned to keep him ignorant as long as possible. As long as he thought she might be physically dangerous, he would be careful. He talked a good game, but inside he was a coward; that was one of the things Valerie's new talent had shown her.

Basically she saw past externals to essentials. It made her a visual clairvoyant according to the DPS tech who'd assessed her as a B8 and assigned her twelve weeks of paid training, but her mentor said her particular variant was unusual. Most clairvoyants saw things or events. Valerie saw truths.

Fortunately for her, there were disciplines helpful to mastering any visual talent. She'd walked away from her last session a week ago with a graduation stamp on her DPS certificate, a career guidebook, and a file full of job listings.

She knew how to identify and interpret what her eyes told

her now. Turning that knowledge into power would be
harder. There was apparently a tremendous demand for sight
that offered insight. She could work with engineers or geolo-
gists, politicians or psychologists—the sheer number of
choices overwhelmed her with what-ifs and the potential for
failure.

Eventually she might find the courage to fill out one of the
applications, but making her work environment more
comfortable was enough for now. Jeff had been a lot less
handsy since learning Valerie was poz and a rollover.

He didn't respond to her taunt now. Instead he squatted
down to put broken china in the tub. Valerie ignored his
muttered *clumsy bitch*. He was helping, and that meant she
could straighten up to ease her aching back muscles before
they locked up. She was still tired, sticky, and embarrassed,
and it didn't feel like much of a victory.

The Marine stared at her from his counter seat. He
knew. He knew he was dying, and he knew Valerie could
see it. Her gaze went to his insignia. Private First Class
Fredericks wasn't from 29 Palms after all. The badges were
for Oasis Company, Mercury Battalion. That unit only
accepted factor-positives whose rollovers brought them
powers too dangerous to entrust to the civilian training
programs.

The median age for rollover was fifty-five. Fredericks
couldn't be more than twenty. Early onset meant early
burnout—that was the death sentence he carried around
inside himself.

Valerie stood up and spoke around the lump that swelled
in her throat. "Order whatever you like," she said, because
food was all she could give him. "It's on me."

"It sure is on you," he said with a flashing grin. His wink at the stains on Valerie's uniform made her smile in spite of herself. "Here," he added, "let me help."

A column of water fountained up from the mess on the floor, becoming a miniature cyclone that scooped everything off the floor and left the tile dry. Jeff squeaked in surprise and sat back on his ass. The waterspout deposited the remaining food and dishes in the bus tub, whirled across Valerie's feet with a cool kiss of wetness that lifted away the soaked-in coffee, then dove into the tub. A small wave splashed over the crotch of Jeff's trousers before the rest disappeared.

Valerie dropped her wet towel onto the dishes. Jeff scrabbled away crabwise. The wet patch made it look like he'd wet himself. Valerie carried the tub away to the kitchen so she didn't burst out laughing in his face.

"Thanks," she said to Private Fredericks.

Jeff followed her through the swinging door, but instead of cornering her and yelling, he returned to the grill. "You take care of him," he said as he picked up the scraper. "He's your kind. Stay away from us." Then he yelled through the serving window, "Nance, you get Val's tops and tips. She's taking the bar."

When Valerie came out, the Marine was sitting alone at the counter with one eyebrow arched and a smile held tight between his lips. He'd obviously overheard the whole conversation. Nancy hurried away to check on the booth who'd lost their food. Valerie silently wished her luck. The school rowdies were one of the few groups who hadn't left after the Marine's power demonstration. They were giggling and snapping pictures a lot more obviously than they thought they were.

Private Fredericks thanked Valerie when she set a mug of coffee in front of him beside a glass of water. She said, "Sorry for the fuss. I mean it, about the food. You didn't have to out yourself in front of everyone like that just to help me."

"Oh, I live for those moments," he said. "I love watching assholes—sorry, ma'am—jerks like that man trip over themselves to get out of my way. I'm juvenile and incorrigible, or so my CO tells me."

He had a smile like Gary's. He was brown, not fair like Valerie's baby boy, and his eyes were dark instead of twinkly pale, but it was the same kind of bold grin full of crooked teeth and pure mischief.

Valerie's heart fell into a bottomless pit. For the first time in her life she finally understood all the horrible fads her mother had inflicted on her in the vain hope of lowering her R-factor risk. It had been done out of ignorance yes, but also from a primal fear born in love—the same reason Valerie had kept her Poz status secret these last years. She would do anything to save her son from this man's fate. *Anything.*

She said, "What'll you have?" and waved at the menu board.

"Steak and eggs'll hit the spot," he said. "Been driving since dawn. Can't tell you how good it is to see a friendly face, and after I went and got you in trouble, too. You're a sweetheart, thanks."

Valerie added a few extras to his order slip and stuck it on the spinner. "Order in." Then she leaned forward and lowered her voice. "Sometimes I wish I wasn't so sweet. You made my day with that splash."

"Well, good." Fredericks buried his smile in a sip of his coffee, then looked around, nodding greetings to the brave few souls willing to meet his eyes. His cup clinked on the saucer, and he gave Valerie a more thoughtful look. "You're what, a clairvoyant? It's something eyes-on. Yours flashed real bright when I came in. And I bet you're still fresh, cuz you looked like you saw a ghost. You can see I'm hitting burnout, huh?"

Valerie flushed. Polite people didn't discuss things like that around here. Maybe in private, when there were no nulls around to make uncomfortable, but never in public.

She glanced at Nancy, who was bussing one of the recently-vacated booths, and then she flung caution to the winds. Maybe she shouldn't care so much about people who didn't respect her. If this soldier barely older than a child could handle a few stares, why couldn't she?

"I'm a diviner, yes," she said. "And new to it. I only passed my field test last week. I came over cool, so I didn't even know I'd rolled until someone told me, and I'm settled at B8. Not too powerful, but yes, I could see you're—you know. I'm sorry."

"I rolled cool too," Fredericks said cheerfully. "Da thought we had a house full of leaky pipes, but the plumber was a low-power waterboy, saw right away it wasn't natural. There was some yelling, and my mama cried a little, and next day I was off to camp for training."

"You poor thing."

"Coulda been worse. One of my squad rolled hot, went start to finish before she knew what hit her. She worked front desk at a car dealership on the coast. Called a fifty-foot wave through the front windows and killed five Porsches. And I'm stronger than her, so it's good I was oriented and in uniform before I peaked. Anyway. What about you? How'd you find out?"

After hearing stories like that, how could she resist sharing her own? "I was at the carnival."

She told her tale and showed Private Fredericks pictures

of her boys, and he was in the middle of another amusing anecdote when Jeff slammed a collection of plates onto the serving shelf. "Order up!"

Nancy grabbed most of the plates and hurried away. Valerie slid a steak, scrambled eggs, toast, hash browns and a fruit bowl in front of Private Fredericks—*after* peering closely at it all to make sure Jeff hadn't added anything nasty.

Describing what she saw with her power was nearly impossible, but she had the knack of it; the food was clean and wholesome. She poured the Marine a glass of juice and refilled his coffee, and then watched in awe as the private inhaled all the food faster than she would've thought possible.

"So you're a diviner, huh?" he said around a mouthful of potato. "That include dowsing? If it does, you should think about the Salton project. That's what brought me out here. I start work tomorrow. You know about that?"

The Salton project was a government water management venture that involved three rivers, four Federal and two state agencies, and an ever-changing cast of administrators and politicians. Someday, the story went, southern California would have its own sustainable water source, large enough to supply both its booming population and vast agricultural investments.

Water had to be found to be managed, which was the reason Valerie had multiple requests from Salton in her collection of job openings. Her ability to sense what lay hidden from sight was exactly what the project managers needed. No amount of dirt or rock would hide water from her, not if she worked in tandem with people who controlled those materials.

"It's in the news all the time up here," Valerie said. "I hear they're hiring in a lot of people. I got some offers in the packet that came with my DPS certificate."

"You don't sound too excited," Fredericks said. "Too far away? Too much paperwork? Don't like salt and mud?"

He grinned with the third guess. Valerie had to swallow and look away again. She didn't have any good excuses. The new dig at the north end would only be an hour commute. She wouldn't even have to drive. There was a shuttle stop downtown to encourage building of new housing developments away from the worksite. Even the lowest salary she'd seen listed would be enough to quit both her current jobs, and she would save on gas and car maintenance if she used the shuttle.

It could change her whole life—and that was what scared her.

How would the boys react to another big change in her life so soon? And her mother? The boys had taken the news of her rollover in stride—although Johnny was disappointed about her lack of a tail—but Mom was barely speaking to Valerie as it was. Keeping the boat of daily life rocking steady was easier than risking new failures. What if a new job didn't work out?

What if she wasn't good enough? She admitted, "I don't know if it's right for me. I've made so many mistakes in the past. If I choose wrong I could screw up my whole future."

Fredericks mopped up a smear of meat juice with a crust of bread and tossed back the last of his coffee in silence. When he wouldn't meet Valerie's eyes, she realized how insensitive she must've sounded. Her new abilities had thrown her life into turmoil, but she at least had a future to worry about.

"I'm sorry," she said. "I didn't think."

He looked up with a smile that glowed from the inside.

"Nah, don't waste tears on me, honey. I was thinking hard, is all. I never thought of it being scary. Me, I've had a good run, and I plan to leave my mark on the world before I go, so Salton's perfect for me. It's gonna be historic."

"What about your family? Don't you want to—?" Valerie stopped when pain licked up like black flames in Frederick's eyes.

"No, ma'am, nobody at home wants me there." He shrugged it off. "That's my other reason for being here. The Corps puts us on terminal leave like it or not, and Salton is offering big bucks for any and all H-series who want to pitch in. I'm H3A. One of the strongest water callers alive right now." He flexed his biceps and struck a pose. "I'll dazzle 'em so much they'll name a ditch after me."

"That's a goal, I guess." Valerie blinked, dazzled by the intensity of the courage Fredericks took for granted. In one dizzy, breathless instant she found in herself what she saw in him, and an idea sparked to life. "Do you have a place to stay yet?"

"No." He slumped down on the stool, all the bravado gone. "I'll scout once I get there. Housing's tight, I know. I can sleep rough outdoors for a bit. Won't be the first time, and it's not like I have to worry about showing up dirty when I check in tomorrow. Everything I own is wash 'n wear, get it?"

Valerie could not allow this kind young man to spend this night or any other sleeping in sand.

Her tiny idea-spark blazed up and became bright determination. "I have a better idea. You'll stay at my place tonight, I'll ride with you to the dig in the morning and get one of those historic jobs for myself. What do you say?"

His brow furrowed, and he frowned. Valerie spoke again before he could protest. "And you'll crash with us until you find a place you can afford, too. My eyes say you're a good man, and I'm supposed to trust my talent. Don't tell me you're scared of *me*."

"Ha! Should I be?" He shook his head, and that fast, he was light and bright again. "Well, I won't say no."

"Good. Let's get out of here." Valerie removed her apron, entered the meal into the cash register and put a twenty in drawer. "Yo, Jeff!" she shouted through the window into the kitchen. "I quit. Happy now?"

Nancy's stricken reaction almost made her feel guilty. Remorse withered away when the woman said, "Quit? Without notice? You can't do that to us."

Watch me. Valerie didn't dare issue that challenge out loud. Burning bridges wasn't in her nature, and trusting her eyes was simpler than trusting this fragile sense of confidence. She took a last look at Nancy's bitter soul and big hairdo, curled her lip at Jeff's fearful cowering, and she marched out the door into her future without saying good-bye.

She should've known it wouldn't be that easy to leave the past behind. Nothing in her life went according to plan. The crash didn't come immediately, no. The happy hopefulness lasted almost another full night before fate's hammer came down on her.

The boys practiced their phone manners on dinner invitations to Lizard-Jen and Purple-Gwen as they'd dubbed their mother's new best friends, and Valerie invited a few of her old friends who were still speaking to her. Gwen brought over her own son, and all the boys ran around shrieking like banshees until Jen threatened to bite them and everyone laughed.

The apartment was so small that a handful of visitors packed it full. The layout—two bedrooms on the outer side of a hall, tiny bathroom and kitchen on the interior, living room at the end—was efficient for a small family, but had no space to spare, and it overheated fast. Every unit in the aging complex had the same problems.

The electrical wiring was too unreliable to support decent air conditioners, and they couldn't get a decent breeze. The balcony doors had been sealed years ago, after the rickety wood balconies were removed.

No one complained, though. There were iced drinks for the adults and ice pops for the kids, and they left the entry door open to the building hall to create a draft. The party clustered in the kitchen, as parties usually did, everyone helping or offering unhelpful suggestions on the best way to put together salads and tacos and bake a frozen pizza.

The meal was made with groceries Private Fredericks had insisted on buying after he said, "Call me Dante, ma'am. You're doing a lot for me already. Let me give back a little, please."

A few drinks into the dinner preparations one of Valerie's high school cronies teased him about his literary name. That led to an unexpected discussion of poetry and drama in which many puns were made, more laughter ensued and the children heard, *we'll explain when you're older* a lot.

Mom sat sullen and silent in her recliner with a tray the whole time, ignoring all attempts to include her in conversation. She'd done that most evenings since Valerie's rollover, but not even her frowning unhappiness could spoil the party mood.

The time passed quickly, with the conversation kept light and many assurances issued that Valerie would have her pick of jobs as a professional at Salton. She memorized every one of those promises, because with every passing hour she wondered harder if she had made the right choice.

Once the guests left, the boys were far too wound up for sleep. Valerie was ready to smother them with their pillows when Dante came to the bedroom door with a stack of the clean dinner dishes Valerie had left to air-dry despite Mom's grumbling about germs and clutter.

"I have little brothers," Dante said, and he looked so wistful that Valerie waved him into the room.

"You can have these two," she said, only half-joking.

"Not SLEEPY!" Johnny announced, and he bounced on the upper bunk so hard Valerie was afraid he would fall off. Gary pulled the covers over his head in the lower one and started to wail. Dante sat on the floor and placed two cups on plates. "Every minute you hooligans sit still and quiet," he said, "I'll add a layer."

Water burbled up in the cups, then jumped from cup to plate to cup, splashing high without ever overflowing. Johnny climbed down and curled up beside his brother, which gave Gary enough courage to peek. They sat very still while Dante built ever-taller creations for the water to dance through, balancing each addition with moving streams of liquid. It was a marvel to watch, but Valerie decided to take advantage of the respite to get her mother settled.

Mom was in a mood. She fussed about brushing her teeth, she whined about being helped with the toilet, and then she decided to be chatty while Valerie put up her hair for the night. "It's bad enough that you're poz," she grumbled. "I'm trying to be tolerant, and you know I love you, but do you have to bring those freaks here all the time? And now you're inviting men overnight while the boys are at home? Honestly, Val."

"Honestly, Mom, what's wrong with you? He's sleeping on the couch, and you know it. You're the one who taught me the Bible verse about hospitality to strangers."

Mom sniffed. "People like him don't deserve charity."

Rather than pick apart all the nastiness packed up in that statement, Valerie said, "That was mean, Mom. I know you're tired, and you've been trying hard, so please, let's not fight."

"I called John Senior," Mom said a minute later. "And I told him. About you being poz and rolling active."

"Oh, Mom. How could you do that?"

"They're his children too, so I thought he had a right to know about the diagnosis."

"He has no rights. He gave them up." Valerie knelt beside the bed and took Mom's hands in her own. "Is this why you've been so unhappy lately?"

Chills ran up her spine and down her arms, leaving sweat in their wake. Her ex-husband was a criminal and a drug addict, but he was also suave and charming. People made excuses for him even when he robbed them blind. "Don't you remember why we left, Mom? He hit me. He hit Johnny. We're not supposed to have any contact. There's a restraining order. I explained this. Why would you reach out?"

Mom's eyes filled with tears. "I know it was a mistake, now. I thought he deserved to know, but he didn't care. He only demanded things and wouldn't listen at all. But you kept flaunting yourself, and I was so angry. You should've been more humble."

Of course the mistake was Valerie's fault. She sighed. "What did he want?"

"He wanted me to say you were unfit, and he sent me papers, but I wouldn't sign because you're not unfit. You're not. You're a good mother, as good as you can be. I know that."

"Well, thank God for that," Valerie said, and her mother kept on talking.

"He called when the papers didn't come back, and he yelled at me and said no dirty poz would raise any sons of his. You are poz, and he had a right to know, but oh, why couldn't you you pretend to be normal?" Mom's voice turned resentful and bitter. "Everything was fine before all this happened."

Valerie helped her mother into bed like always without saying another word, and then she retreated to the living room. Anxiety made her head ache, but she dredged up her courage and listened to Dante murmur and her boys laugh while she wrote a note to the too-expensive lawyer who had arranged her divorce. She would hope for the best.

Even if DPS didn't have legal clout with Family Services, her husband had acted badly enough in public, that he wouldn't get custody easily. Charm only went so far. She would fight John even harder than she had in the divorce, when she'd first learned that she had a backbone after all. Her backbone was stronger now.

The note was done, and Dante's bedding was ready on the couch before the boys fell asleep. The Marine rolled up in the blankets on the couch fully-clothed, and Valerie went to her bedroom and stared at the dark ceiling for hours while Mom snored in the other bed and her fears clamored loudly at her.

She escaped into unsettled dreams and woke to the strident beeping of smoke alarms, and she thought it was a nightmare until she sat up. Harsh smoke clogged her nose and throat, tasting of ash and stinging tears from her eyes. A crackling roar filled the darkness with fearful noise. She reached for the lamp switch. Nothing happened. The room remained pitch black.

Johnny screamed, "MOMMY!"

She was out of bed and heading for the boys before she was awake enough to think *the building is burning* and remember her fire drill training. Was the bedroom door cool? Too late, she was past it. Should she be standing up? No. Her lungs felt heavy, and spots floated in her vision. She dropped to her hands and knees, then lower, and gasped for air.

The stench of gasoline joined the reek of smoke, and the hall was hot and blacker than black, but not hot enough to kill her in the doorway. With a wrench of willpower Valerie peered *through* the darkness. The apartment layout lit up as if traced in lines of light, and a hellish glow suffused all the invisible walls on the interior: *danger, get away, get away.* There would be no escape down the fire stairs at the end of the building.

Valerie moved on her elbows, gasping, and her lungs filled with the acrid heat. The few feet to the boys room seemed like a million miles. Her sight deserted her, and embers bit and stung her bare arms.

One thought stayed cool and clear: get to Johnny and Gary.

A figure loomed out of the blackness, surrounded by a pale eerie glow. When Valerie screamed, she couldn't hear her own voice. Dante crouched and caught her by the arms. "Front door is blistering," he shouted in her ear. "Wall's burning through."

He couldn't know Valerie knew that. She shouted back, "Boys' room! Fire ladder!" and led the way. Orange tongues of flames licked through the roiling smoke in the entryway behind them, lighting up a thick gray cloud above her. She flinched from the heat inside the bathroom as she crawled past.

Johnny and Gary were hiding under their bed, too frightened to move. Valerie didn't question how she knew they were there. She *saw*, and she grabbed them while Dante crawled onward, and they clung to her as she made her way to the window behind him. Hot, gritty water squished under her elbows and knees.

Glass shattered, and the smoke boiled outside and let in fresh air. Valerie took a strained breath that turned into coughs. She pointed to the toy chest. Dante grabbed the rope ladder, anchored it and shook it out. Then he peeled the boys off Valerie one by one, his every touch a wet caress, and gently lowered them through the window.

The boys practiced with that ladder every month, and they scuttled down it without hesitation once they got started. Valerie watched them until they were safe on the ground.

Waiting hands gathered them in, and someone called upwards, but she couldn't understand a word. Lights flashed everywhere, and all the voices were a jumble of shouts. People milled in a crowd of nightgowns and bare chests and blankets, faces tilted upwards, mouths gaping open, fingers pointing. They were painted in reds and oranges, blues and white from the flashing emergency lights and the glow of the fire.

Valerie shook like a leaf, overwhelmed, and horror wrapped around her chest so tight she could not cough. Her children were safe—but they were safe because she'd not thought even for an instant about her own mother. "Oh, God, no. Mom. Oh, *Mom*."

Wood splinters stabbed her fingertips as her nails bit into the windowsill, and she sobbed, because she could not face that hallway again, could not even turn around to look at it.

The smoke in the room flickered with an evil bright glow; the fire was eating across the hall. The shadows danced and wavered. She could not move. She could not leave her mother in that hell.

Dante embraced her, his arms damp and cool, and the roar of the flames was so loud she heard his shout as a whisper. "Go, ma'am. Go on. The boys need you. I'll take care of your mom."

She couldn't move, but when Dante put her hands on the ladder, her body moved on its own. When she reached the bottom rung, she was surrounded and pushed back and forth by kind hands that wrapped her fingers around a bottle of water, flashed lights in her face and wiped it clean, and finally reunited her with her boys.

Johnny climbed up her leg to bury his face against her hip, and she hefted Gary in both arms before she turned back, head tilted up and gaping like all the rest. The building was edged and crowned in leaping flames now, gold and yellow against the black smoke and the white sprays of hoses. She'd never imagined how loud and bright a fire could be, how swiftly it could spread. A whimper caught hoarse in her throat, coarse with fear, clawing her with guilt.

People were still coming out the front door, out the fire stairs at either end of the building. All around, jets of water rose, and ladders went up from trucks. The streams of water wavered and split, multiplied and augmented by poz elementals on the fire department team, while their air and fire specialists smothered and killed the blazing embers that leaped to other roofs. Despite their best efforts, the top floor —Valerie's floor—was fully engulfed in flames. Like the other buildings being doused with preventative measures, the unit was older than the fire codes, and its wood frame was desert-dry.

Her mother was up there. "Mom," she whispered, "God, please, not Mom."

Conversations fell around her along with the hot flicks of ash and the mist from the fire hoses.

It went up so fast!

What happened?

Does anyone know how it started?

Is everyone out?

Valerie knew the answer to the last question: no. Her mother wasn't the only one trapped in the building. She could see lives through the walls, tiny sparks in the smoke. Her whole body tightened, willing them all to move, for them to descend safe and sound.

None did. No shuffling woman with gray hair in curlers appeared at the fire door, no tall, dark man who glowed like death, no one at all emerged from the inferno. They were all on the third floor, trapped above flame, inside flame.

A commotion stirred the crowd of neighbors and onlookers to her left, offering a glimpse of the building entrance. A pair of firefighters dragged out a man whose feet scraped on the ground. They threw him at the waiting police in blue uniforms and clean, flat-brimmed hats. The murmurs of conversation shifted, carrying cold news.

Him?

On purpose? How do they know?

Look at that. Do you think he tried to burn himself up too?

I hope he dies.

Valerie was not sure if she heard that last whisper or if she only thought it. She knew that man's jutting cheekbones even when they were bristling with thick beard stubble. She knew his voice when she heard it badgering the police with reminders about rights, complaining of injuries and informing them how soon they would regret messing with him.

She knew John's face, and the soul shining through his skin was even more twisted now than when she'd first seen it with her powerful new vision. Her stomach heaved, and she knelt to hide the boy's faces, so they wouldn't see their father being dragged away in handcuffs.

If he couldn't have them, no one could; that was how his mind worked, with no thought at all for the other lives he endangered. They all deserved to die, he was shouting now, so lost in his sickness that he thought that incriminating himself was a defense.

It was Valerie's fault, for leaving him, for lying to him about being a monster, for keeping his sons from him. It was her fault, he screamed, until one of the paramedics touched him on the forehead and let him fall unconscious to the ground.

Then he was strapped onto a gurney and driven off by his police escorts. Valerie let the sick feelings drain out of her, into the muddy earth at her feet, but the screams echoed in her head. Doubts stirred, awakened by the accusations. Was this her fault?

The night roared, and the garish light from the burning building vanished beneath a huge, moving mass of blackness. Valerie's ears popped. Everything went quiet between breaths before the crowd noise surged up louder than ever, with people shouting exclamations and happy comments across each other until they sounded like a flock of gulls fighting over a piece of bread.

A fishy scent came to Valerie on a wet breeze, tasting of

salt, and she stared at the smoking building. With the flames extinguished, the blue and white lights on the emergency vehicle cast new and deeper shadows now, but the foamy water still cascading down the siding was bright as day to her, phosphorescent with power. The gull-noises of the crowd whirled around her.

It smells like ocean.

It's a miracle.

Did you hear a helicopter?

How did they get so much water here so fast?

"He brought it," Valerie whispered. She set down Gary and grabbed his hand and Johnny's. She ran with them, stumbling and pushing her way past neighbors and strangers towards the tall, thin, glowing man carrying Mom out the fire door.

Dante set Mom down on the bottom step before he staggered and dropped. Other people ran or limped or staggered out the door past him.

He'd said he would take care of Mom, and he'd kept his promise. The cost shimmered in his eyes, and it blazed through his body so fiercely that Valerie could see it killing him from yards away.

The crowd came shouting forward, but they fell back again at the orders of firefighters and medics who brought oxygen masks and blankets and helping hands. All the victims were hurried out of harm's way, until only a few first responders stood there, helpless in the face of suffering they could not ease. With them stood Mom, leaning heavily on a firefighter's arm and crying her eyes out.

Valerie didn't question the way the crowd parted for her, nor the way the first responders broke ranks to let her join them. She didn't question Gary allowing himself to be scooped into a stranger's arms, or Johnny holding tight to his brother's hand as he released hers. She didn't question any of it, because she needed to be there too much to think of anything else.

"Hey," Dante whispered when he saw her. Ocean surf crashed in his eyes, and death rolled under his smile. Valerie blinked back tears, and Dante said, "Looks like I won't be giving you that ride to work after all."

Words wouldn't come. She swallowed tears and mouthed a voiceless thank you. Dante laughed, low in his chest, as much a little boy in that moment as Valerie's were, and then he dipped his chin in a pleased nod.

"Told you I'd make my mark before I was done," he said. "This'll do."

He stopped breathing then, the inner light died with him, and his flesh dissolved into the dirt. A moment later, a tiny burble of water welled up and began to trickle across the lawn.

"I will go anyway," Valerie whispered, and all the lingering doubts ran down into the earth with her tears. "I will."

How could she do anything else, after this?

She let the cool new water roll over her fingers, fresh and sweet, and she put her hand over her heart and swore she would not waste the gift she'd been given. She would climb on that shuttle to Salton, she would face the unknown with all the strength she could muster, and she would never, *ever* forget what honor looked like.

The world crashed back, surrounding her with noisy commotion and confusion. Johnny came running back and cried against her leg because she was crying, while Gary stood silent and hiccuped around the fist he was chewing on.

Mom coughed and hobbled closer. "He did good," she said in a hoarse voice.

Valerie shook her head. That was the highest compliment Mom ever offered, and she'd bestowed it on a man she barely accepted as human. "Nice, Mom. Real nice. Would you say that to his face if he was alive?"

"Yes." Mom said the word without inflection, but something made Valerie turn to see her. The truth left her stunned, and Mom said, "I would try."

It was a choked whisper like a babe's first cry, a first, feeble attempt at something new. Sometimes the best wasn't enough, even when it was all someone had. Sometimes the smallest effort could change everything.

"That's good." Valerie took a deep breath of ocean-scented air that would always remind her of this night, and she opened her eyes wide, to let life amaze her with all the good things still in it. "That's all any of us can ever do."

THE LETTER

THIS IS the letter that R-factor carriers dread receiving. Its arrival means—at best—your life as you know it is over. You're about to become a social outcast who may face verbal harassment, physical harm, and social rejection for the rest of your living days.

At worst it's a death sentence couched in bureaucratic double-speak.

DEAR <NAME>

Your Ackerman-Chung R-factor activation test result for the year <YEAR> is: POSITIVE.

Your name, status, and Federal identification number have been forwarded to the Department of Public Safety, and you will report to the nearest Adaptation & Placement Facility by <DATE> at the latest.

Failure to comply will result in legal
action and involuntary internment in accor-
dance with Federal legislation referencing
Ackerman-Chung deviation and Public Safety
jurisdiction. (ref: FL1834-87/1981, FL
2543/1981)

A list of available facilities is attached.
All efforts will be made to accommodate your
preferred choice, but vacancies at the time
of your internment and the nature of your
transition may require transfer to any DPS-
certified facility. (note 1)

Prepare for a stay of one to twelve months.
If further training and/or containment is
deemed warranted by the personnel in charge
of your transition, you may at any point be
remanded to the custody of the Department of
Defense, USMC Mercury Battalion, for additional training in compliance with appropriate laws. (FL729-87/1943, FL 11/1959)
(note 2)

The DPS highly recommends a visit your local
Administration office at your earliest
convenience. Specialists there can determine
how best the Department can meet your and
your family's needs and will assist you with
transition paperwork and all necessary
travel arrangements. Appeals for hardship
exemptions can be filed at that time. Due to

the unpredictability of transition outcomes, all active R-factor citizens are encouraged to put personal and financial affairs in order before reporting in.

If no DPS office exists within reasonable distance (refer to FL803-66/1946 for specifics) then you may access the national DPS hotline for assistance with any questions. Under the above circumstances you **must also sign and return** this letter in the enclosed envelope to any United States Postal Service Facility to confirm its receipt.

You remain responsible for reporting to one of the DPS Adaptation facilities on the attached list before the date listed above. Payment vouchers for public transportation will be provided via the USPS. (FL2591-14/1962) (note 3)

All arriving program participants may bring one (1) small suitcase up to 2000 cubic inches for clothing and personal effects. A list of prohibited items is attached. Additional FAQ materials can be found online. Meals, bedding, appropriate training equipment, medicines, (note 4) and personal hygiene supplies will be provided by DPS personnel for the duration of your stay.

If returning this letter as your official
registration, please list your preferences
below so staff can better accommodate your
needs during your time in DPS custody:

Room: smoking/non-smoking

Meals: vegetarian/vegan/ other diet
(please specify)

The Department of Public Safety thanks
you for your cooperation.
Regards,
<NAME>

Central Office of Adaptation & Placement
United States Department of Public Safety.

ATTACHMENTS:
Adaptation Facilities currently open to
(continental US) Prohibited Personal Effects
List

NOTES:
(1) Due to uneven geographic dispersion,
there may be no facility vacancies in your
immediate vicinity. Facilities have been
listed in increasing geographic distance
from your address. Transportation will be
provided at no cost by all common carriers.
Not all facilities are suitable for all
types of transitions.

(2) Military supervision of no less than one
(1) year is compulsory for certain power
classes. Please check with your local DPS
office or the national website for the
current listings. These designations cannot
be legally appealed.

(3) Postal records indicate you do NOT
qualify for assistance from the national
hotline. Be aware there are substantial fees
associated for unauthorized access of this
service. If you believe your case is not
being handled well by your local DPS office,
please file a complaint online or through
the USPS. Forms available on request.

(4) All personal medical records will be
forwarded to the appropriate DPS personnel
upon receipt of this release.

POWERHOUSE

COLONEL MARCIA GALLOWAY opened the door carefully, much as she wanted to slam it to the wall. She hadn't come a thousand miles from home on a moment's notice to throw a tantrum. She had a crisis to contain.

Preventable disasters aggravated her more than anything else in the world, but the world did not care if her temper was hot enough to melt steel. Emotion caused disasters. Cool reason resolved them.

She forced the burning rage inward where it would only cramp her muscles and rot holes in her stomach. A little of the heat must have reached her eyes despite her efforts. The two technicians fussing over a table full of recording equipment stood up so fast that one woman tipped over her chair before Marcia could get out the words, "As you were."

A gesture dismissed the techs. Another sharp motion shut the door—*gently*—in their wake. Two measured steps covered the distance to a window into the adjoining interview room. She righted the fallen chair and gripped the back as hard as she dared. Cool plastic dug into her palms while she catalogued the elements of this disaster.

The room was a standard twelve-by-twelve, with the exit door on the right. Gray tile floor, gray extruded paneling on the walls. Two wood chairs and a metal table pushed to one side. Notepad computer on the table. Fluorescent lights hanging overhead. Single air duct high on one wall.

A typical interview venue, but for some members of the population, a typical room might as well be a medieval dungeon. One of those individuals was sitting on a foam mat against the far wall.

Corporal Jack Coby topped eight feet in height, which made the ceiling a standing hazard. The chairs would have collapsed under his weight. His uniform was soaked in sweat because the ventilation couldn't keep up with the heat his body generated, and his face was buried in his arms to hide his eyes from a glare he would find unbearably bright.

The man's physical limitations were a matter of public record, and his rights were protected by federal law. This was the kind of situation that sank military careers and started Senate investigations.

"Hello, disaster," Marcia said.

The other occupant of the room passed in front of the window, offering a fine view of broad shoulders trapped inside an immaculate service uniform. In other company, Captain Malik Jefferson would be considered tall, even powerful. He had little room to pace, but he kept trying, and his attention never left the man in the corner.

Marcia confirmed that the recorders were on. Then she slapped the intercom switch. "Do you have any idea how big a bucket of civil rights shit you're standing in, Captain? Are you engaged in neglect or outright torture? You can't claim ignorance. I conducted your Mercury unit orientation myself, so I know you're up to speed on accommodation law."

Captain Jefferson gave the observation window a long, silent look. Gray hair at his temples added a touch of maturity to a face that would always look younger than its age, and lips that fell naturally into a smiling bow more than canceled out the severity of his tight regulation haircut.

Marcia knew his affable expression masked a temper that matched her own for intensity, and she saw warning signs of it in his eyes now. Jefferson picked up the notepad and slammed its screen flat against the window at eye level. Then he slid it downward several inches to Marcia's eye level. He might be new to Mercury Battalion, but he'd been a platoon commander in the Corps before his career intermission. He knew how to deliver a fuck-you-sir message up the chain with flair.

The consent waiver on display brought down the scale of the disaster by several orders of magnitude. Coby had waived his legal rights, including those entitling him to reasonable environmental adjustments.

Captain Jefferson said, "Where would you have me put him, ma'am? I only have enough T-series brig cells for six. Don't blame me, blame the base architects who never imagined needing enough space for a whole flipping squad of Tees."

He paused, and his shoulders sagged. "This was the best I could do, but I'm well aware the Battalion can't afford bad press this close to the appropriations vote. I'll sign over and resign if that's what needed, ma'am. Are you here to take over as investigating officer?"

"I am not." Marcia smiled, safe in the knowledge that the indulgence couldn't be seen. Jefferson might be as green as spring grass when it came to the eccentricities of his new command, but his readiness to sacrifice himself for the good of the unit was heartwarming. "I am here to help. This isn't a witch hunt, captain. I'm not only here as Mercury Command. I'm also the Battalion's ranking Public Safety rep. That's my top hat in this situation."

The Department of Public Safety designation gave Marcia authority over all other military and civilian agencies in this case. Within a restricted sphere of influence, DPS officials had the right to gather evidence, level charges, adjudicate and pass sentence. It was an obscene amount of power to invest in individuals, but the government had tried worse strategies over the years.

Marcia said, "Think of it as joint custody. Your investigation with my oversight and logistical support from my DPS civilian team. And thank your lucky stars I know you aren't really a sadistic bigot, because I could sink your career over what I'm seeing here."

Jefferson frowned around the room. "What's the issue? I can't make the place bigger."

So it was ignorance after all. Marcia might have guessed. Mercury Battalion caught a lot of rare power variants. "He's T5-Y, Captain. The Y variant is tricky in combination. T-Y's are photosensitive and heat sensitive. See to his needs while I look over your preliminary findings, and we'll forget it ever happened."

"Aye-aye, ma'am. Thank you. That variant chart is worse than any Table of Organization." Jefferson turned on the silent corporal. "Dammit, Jackass. I asked if you were comfortable. I don't waste time on empty courtesies."

Corporal Coby replied in a deep voice too slurred for Marcia to understand his words. Jefferson apparently had no trouble. "When I ask any direct question in the future, you will answer it fully or face unpleasant consequences. Clear?"

Rumble.

Marcia glanced at the transcriber unit. Its filters and algorithms could pull intelligible data from a wide range of audio input—a necessity when dealing with soldiers whose voices might drift into the ultrasonic or subsonic range depending on how their powers manifested.

The words "aye, aye, sir," popped up onscreen.

While Jefferson oversaw the room improvements Marcia caught up on the few developments that had occurred since she first received the case alert. When the captain came into Observation, she waved him into the chair facing hers.

"Tell me if I'm missing anything," she said. "At 03:30 today, Dormitory 2, squad bay B literally came off its foundation. Choke-out sanctions deployed automatically in response to the pheromone spike. Clearly something threw the entire squad into berserker mode, but ten hours and three interview rotations later, you still have no idea what incited the rampage. Corporal Coby there claimed responsibility, but he refuses to elocute."

"That's the pathetic sum of it." Jefferson frowned at the floor. "I have suspicions and forensics. It's a rough crowd except for the two newest reboots. You saw the page 11s?"

"I did. I read all their jackets on the flight out." Marcia clenched her fists to keep her anger contained. Human beings had been abusing each other in the name of discipline long before any of them began changing into something else at midlife. That made it no easier to accept. "You think a blanket party set off a violent cascade?"

"I think worse. Coby refused medical. It is a T-series prerogative, but they were all bloody wrecks by the time they dropped, and he's the only one who waived intervention. Problem is, I can't charge on a hunch." Jefferson hit the intercom switch. "Hey, Jackass, I'm done listening to silence. Relax and enjoy the shade until your next wellness check. Maybe you'll feel chatty once your belly's full."

Rumble.

"No, you can't decline that. You can duck the full exam, but the vitals checks and extra chow are compulsory."

Rumble-rumble.

"Of course I'll come back even though the lights are off, if you're ready to talk. Do you think I'm scared of the dark?"

The exasperation in his tone danced close to anger. Marcia leaned over to cut the intercom. "Ease off, Captain. He doesn't mean to be insulting. He was early onset, and he's under a lot of stress."

"That doesn't excuse insubordination."

"It isn't insubordination." Marcia placed her hand flat on the table and pressed hard. "It's a testament to your leadership that he thinks you *might* join him in a blacked-out room. Look." She lifted her palm. "You cannot know what this does to people."

Jefferson eyed the smoking imprint without flinching. "I can try. Go on."

"I'm a P1K: pyrokinetic, top power grade. The K is for telekinesis, in case you've forgotten that variance too. A T9, the weakest in Coby's series, could cross my effective range and kill me before she noticed I'd burned her guts away, and she would survive the experience. I wouldn't."

"If you're saying I should be too scared to interview him, you're wasting your time."

"No. If I thought you scared easily, you wouldn't have this post." Marcia searched for better words. "I want you to understand *his* mindset better. I rolled at forty-three under close supervision. Ten years on, I still terrify myself on bad days. Coby killed three people in his first rampage episode at the age of fourteen. He will not outgrow that horror. He will never forget it."

"He's feeling self-doubt, not implying cowardice," Jefferson said after a moment's thought.

"Yes."

Jefferson's ready empathy was the main reason Marcia had approved his transfer to this post, why she'd tapped a power-less man to lead the most dangerous unit of monsters in a battalion dedicated to them. "Most EO's bolt after one hitch, if they live that long. They want to get the most out of their short lives. The ones who re-enlist do it because Corps discipline is all that makes them feel human enough to walk in the world. Coby has re-upped twice. Find out what happened in that dorm, Captain. Find out how the Corps failed him."

"That's my plan." Jefferson keyed the intercom again. "I'm coming in, Jackass. Don't trip me, or I'll put you on mess duty for a month."

BRIG INTERVIEW ROOM 1
14:40S 11 MAY

Glare slashed across Jack's eyes and stabbed right into his brain. He grunted as his strained neck muscles locked into cramps, and then he swallowed blood. The empty tooth sockets were finally starting to bud.

Darkness returned. Captain Jefferson waited near the closed hatch. Jack could see him clearly. He didn't have the superb hearing of a B-variant, or the sensitive nose of a W, but he had the full T-series visual spectrum.

The captain was standing next to the damned bench. "You're still on the deck," the captain said. "The work detail brought in a bench from Barracks 3 for you."

"I know, sir." Jack's heart stuttered, and he started to sweat again. His chest and thighs ached. The bruising was hours gone, but he could still sense the cold pressure of waffled metal, feel the slam of the rounded edge against muscle and the scrape of tile under his knees.

He would pick up the bench and break it, if the captain ordered him onto it. Better yet, he would break the captain with it. He wouldn't even need both hands. His fingers would meet on the far side of the man's neck. One. Little. Squeeze.

Adrenaline surged. The aches faded. His calves twitched, and so did the long muscles in his back, always the first ones to respond. *Run. Fight. Move. Hit. Hurt. Punish.*

He overcame the reaction with a wrench of willpower and got the breathless panting under control. Darkness made it easier. In the dark there was no failure, no pain, no screams. Darkness was safe.

"Heavy breathing is not talking." The captain sat down on the bench. "I will find out what sent your squad into uncontrolled rampage, Corporal. Two can keep a secret if one is dead, that's the saying. There's nine of you, and I'm told Tees can survive a nuke hit given sufficient healing time and supportive care. You had Cooper's brains on your knuckles, but the docs swear he'll live. Someone will talk. No one's going to die."

Jack's headache throbbed along with his pulse. Oh,

someone would die. He would see to that. All he had to do was keep his mouth shut and wait.

Before his chance came he might get busted down and pull heavy brig time for the destroyed barracks, but property damage was still only a summary charge. He would see justice done once he was back on duty.

He'd managed a false statement earlier to get things moving, but the waiting part was hard. He couldn't bring himself to lie again, and he didn't know what else to do.

The captain said, "It's freezing in here, and you are wasting my time. Maybe I should warm up with a walk over to sick bay and check on Private Stanislav. What do you think of her?"

Jack ran his tongue over his remaining teeth. *Direct question. Speak.* "She'll make a good Marine, once the boot polish wears off. First to volunteer, last to complain."

The captain said, "Of course she's eager. She wants to complete her compulsory hitch with a bonus, pass her control tests and go home to her kids. Who wouldn't? She's a good woman. Not the kind to nag her squad leader."

A howl came up Jack's throat and stuck there. *I should've noticed. I should've known there would be trouble.* He choked down the guilt, but memories came up again on a surge of nausea and adrenaline. He couldn't stop the shakes this time. His vision hazed red at the edges. Muscles prickled and twitched.

"You need to leave, sir," he said. "I request a control exemption. Please, go."

"Request denied," the captain said. "We'll get through this together. Don't worry about talking. Just relax, close your eyes and listen to a little bedtime story."

All the words made sense, but not *sense,* and the deck

crumbled between Jack's claws when he grabbed at the tiles. His pulse hammered in his ears, in his gut, in his bones, and his hands gouged furrows into the concrete flooring.

The captain snapped, "Relax. That was an order, Marine. Sit back. Eyes shut."

The rising tide of emotion slammed into the solid necessity of obedience. Jack put his hands in his lap and bowed his aching head, and he closed his eyes as ordered. "I'm listening, sir," he whispered.

"This is a story about my grand-daddy," said the captain. "He was a Marine too, way back in WWII. People called his grand-daddy property, but the Marines gave Pappy a rifle and made him one of the few and proud. You know much history?"

"Not much, sir." He hadn't tried for education points in years. Waste of time, the registrars told him. Early onset. Sure to die before the Corps got its investment back. "I know the Corps was different then."

"All male, for one thing. All white, for another. Mostly young, too. A unit of black men? That was revolutionary. I wonder sometimes, where we would be today if the President's cousin hadn't hit onset in the middle of a state dinner. But she did roll over, and so did a hundred thousand others between '43 and '45. Eighty percent of that first wave were women, and a huge share of them were T, R and P powerhouses who rolled hot and wreaked havoc."

"Like I did."

"In principle." The captain paused, shifted his weight. "FDR signed the orders to form Mercury Battalion to manage the need for troops on American soil, and the Corps took on the task of training volunteers who could fight fire with fire. Literally, in some cases. Those women and men kept the home front safe so the rest of the country could win the war, because the changes of First Night hit everywhere, of course."

The portable AC unit ticked over in the silence. The darkness behind Jack's eyelids wasn't red now, and the prickling eased. His brain felt foggy, and he wondered if he had missed a question. Was he supposed to speak?

The captain said, "Would you ever think a woman was an inferior soldier because of her plumbing? I doubt it, but it was assumed, once upon a time. Not so long ago, dark skin meant you weren't human to some folks. Sexuality was a *thing*, as my niece would say. Only seventy years ago. Plenty of places that's still true, but now a third of the population changes color, sprouts new parts, or develops weird talents midway through life. Half the civilian reboots in Mercury don't even look human. The ratio runs 60-40 women to men. Do you think any of that changes what it means to be a Marine?"

That one, Jack could answer without hesitation. "No, sir. It does not."

"Indeed it does not, Corporal. You are a good Marine, and we both know what that means. A good Marine would never let criminals walk free so that he could plot his own private revenge. Not even if the criminals deserve worse than hanging."

Jack's head snapped back from shock. Paneling crunched, and he saw snowy white, bleeding red. His breath came fast again, but he held on. *Wait. Wait and say nothing. He doesn't know. He can't.*

He waited.

Captain Jefferson waited.

The waiting tied Jack in knots, inside.

The captain spoke again at last, so softly ."Let me tell you another story. You just listen, and you tell me if I get it wrong," "Got it?"

"Aye, sir."

"There's a Marine. He's not very smart, and he's only a kid in a service that midlines at age 50 now, but he still elbows his way up to E-4 in a unit where promotions don't come easy or often. His rank gives him authority over men and women twice his age, ones who hate themselves, ones who would rather be running diners or driving trucks or teaching school. This Battalion is different from the rest of the Corps in one critical way, Corporal. The damned souls assigned to Mercury's cohorts either drill or die. They're only Marines on the outside when they leave the reboot camps. The Corps has to work to make them bleed green. This Marine, he does that for his troops. He leads with his heart. By the way, Gunny Rivera had you listed for an E-5 slot. Did you know?"

That was a knife twist, to learn he'd come so close to making sergeant. "No, sir. Thank you for the information, sir."

"So formal. Where was I? Oh. The Corps does change. It adapts. By land, by sea, now air and space, for instance. The changes to infantry doctrine that come with having brute squads and pyro support could fill libraries. Mercury is of the Corps, but it is unique in the Corps. Do you see my point?"

"I think so, sir." The anxious prickling started again. The captain's point was that certain activities, officially frowned on but universally practiced, would not be tolerated in his house. Typical officer bullshit. Report abuse, they insisted, then punished the ones who complained. Nothing ever changed.

He'd known what they would believe when he took responsibility for the rampage, but it still hurt like being torn into pieces, that his captain believed the lie. "Permission to speak freely, sir?"

"Of course. That is why I'm freezing my balls off in here, corporal. Please do."

"The rampage cascade was my fault, but I would never sanction—" He could not make the words. "*Semper Fidelis.* Faithful to the mission, faithful to each other. We don't turn on our own. Beatings aren't discipline. They're abuse."

"Exactly that." The captain rose to his feet, stood near the dim rectangle of the mirror. "I want to know who broke that faith, Corporal. Who thought might made right? I know it wasn't you. Give me the names of the rabid dogs in your squad, and I swear they will be put down."

What was that promise worth? *Nothing.* "It was my fault, sir. They were my responsibility."

The captain sighed. "You took such drastic injuries last night that you're still bleeding, yet Forensics tells me the clothes turned over to them were clean, like you stripped—or *were* stripped—before you were injured. I won't give you an order you'll refuse, Jackass. I won't push you from obstruction into perjury. You don't have to lie. I'm only asking for the names. Help me keep my oath, Corporal. Don't let the forsworn escape justice."

Jack couldn't get his thick tongue around words without his throat closing up. He shook his head. *It's dark. He can't see you.* "Nothing to say, sir."

After a moment, the captain said, "You know, you basically look like a super-large man. Keep your mouth shut, put your hands in your pockets, and my granddaddy would've said, 'you could pass.' Minimal scute development. That's why you overheat. No brow ridge to protect the eyes, so you're photo-sensitive. The real downside of the Y-variant is that it's in the bottom quartile for muscle power for the T-series, and you're short, relatively speaking. Puts you at a disadvantage when you're attacked by other Tees."

I could still rip you in half. "I wasn't assaulted, sir."

"No? Oh, sorry. Of course not. I wasn't talking about you." The captain prowled around the room again, shadow against shadows. "I was talking about this other Marine again. The one who came across animals tormenting their prey and intervened without hesitation. The one who put himself in harm's way for a sister in arms, like she would've done for him. The Marine who downed at least one armored predator twice his weight before being savaged in turn, before others arrived and took him out—"

"No," Jack heard himself say. "That isn't what happened."

The events didn't sound real, when the captain laid them out in that soft voice, and Jack couldn't let the man trash-talk his good people. "The others were trying to help us, but the blood frenzy, it hit so fast—" He'd bitten his way loose, he'd screamed, the others had come running, and his panic tipped them all over the edge into madness. *Red blood on white tile, red haze, white-hot rage.*

Shame washed up, because he had failed so badly. He was a soldier, not an animal.

The captain's footsteps receded, then returned. He stopped near Jack's feet. "How does this story end, Corporal? Does it end in justice or in greater dishonor? If I put my fairy tale on record and ask for your signature, will I get it? If I make you a list of names, will you mark the right ones? That's all I need, Jackass. Will you help me do my duty?"

It all sounded so reasonable. So distant. So clean. Jack curled up around helpless defeat that tasted like blood and felt like death. Fury and humiliation screamed at him to stay silent, bide his time, take vengeance in the dark.

Honor. Courage. Commitment. He swallowed down the rage. "I will, sir."

BRIG OBSERVATION ROOM 1
17:45S 11 MAY

Marcia couldn't fault Captain Jefferson's dedication. He stayed in the ice-cold room under dimmed lights with Coby and worked through a chow break to help him with his written statement. The corporal threw up the meal before he finished the report, but after cleanup he went straight back to work making corrections and additions. Jefferson stayed with him, offering silent support without judgment.

There were pauses for blank staring and tears, and a second chow break came and went before both men were satisfied with the results. Marcia followed their rumble-and-reply conversation on the transcriber and wondered if dedication had led the captain astray.

The lights went out, and Jefferson returned to Observation. He went straight to the blank, dark window. Marcia gave him a minute alone there before joining him there. The air between them shimmered with heat. Stress still had her running hot, and she had to vent it somehow. If she wanted, she could leave third-degree burns under a victim's unmarked clothes. Jefferson didn't move an inch.

In the minimal illumination, Jefferson's black skin and hair offered no reflection to the glass. Marcia's hair made a gray frame around the barely-visible blur of her face. She kept it short even though Mercury Battalion was exempt from most physical appearance standards. Everything she did set an example, and this message was simple: do all you can.

Some rules could be bent. Some were inviolable. Marcia said, "I'm impressed you were able to connect with him like that."

Jefferson let his chin sink to his chest. "Manipulating a brutalized, desperate young man isn't all that hard, ma'am."

"That wasn't what I meant, and you know it. How did you understand a single word coming out of his mouth? Coby sounds like he's gargling boulders, and you didn't use a transcriber or translator bug. If you ordered one of your F-series telepaths to rip the facts out his brain and relay them to you, then you are toast."

Jefferson snorted. "Please. I may be iffy on variants, but I know the law, ma'am. Telepaths can only be used to *verify* sworn statements. I can swear under oath that none of my fortunetellers invaded Corporal Coby's mental privacy."

Marcia could smell evasion. "Drop the other shoe, Captain."

"I had my own hitchhiker. There's no law against that, although I expect there will be one as soon as someone else thinks of it."

The explanation didn't help. "Start at the beginning."

"This morning it took Coby five minutes repeating bloody spew into a transcriber to get, 'My fault, sir' onto the record. He cried, ma'am, not from the pain but from humiliation. Until that shattered jaw knits fully, he'll sound like a slobbering animal. Consulting a machine every time he opened his mouth—I couldn't do that to him. Not after what I suspected he'd gone though already."

"And a telepathic ride-along was the next idea that sprang to mind?"

"More or less," Jefferson said after a hesitation. "I read somewhere that verbalized ideas sometimes echo through other minds. I asked for a volunteer strong enough to try it. PFC Sharon took the job, if you need to validate my story."

Marcia restrained herself to a nod because dancing a little jig of happiness would be highly inappropriate. Picking up Jefferson and hugging him would be tragically worse, given how hot she was at the moment. She still wanted to skip and leap with joy.

Jefferson had demonstrated more understanding of his command's potential with that one act than some of his predecessors had ever shown. Finally, her problem unit might be getting the leadership it deserved. *Finally.*

Gateway Company had been a thorn in her side since her first day with the Battalion. It was home to the heaviest hitters and brute-strength specialists in the Corps, and it had initially been a plum assignment for career Marine officers. Ambition and skill did not necessarily go hand in hand, however, and the unit's reputation had been eroding for years. Morale failure was devastating, and the results were worse, as demonstrated by today's events.

Mercury Battalion's dispersed homeland deployment made administration a nightmare, and there were no small decisions when minor problems could result in empty riverbeds or artificial earthquakes. Marcia had thrown her best at this unit time and again, only to see them founder on the rocky shores of institutional apathy. Jefferson was already establishing his beachhead.

The captain was eyeing Marcia with uncertainty now. She said, "Detail it in your report for the JAG, and let's move on. My staff will do Coby's verification."

"Aye, aye, ma'am." Jefferson paused for thought. "Moving

on, then. Coby's testimony and forensics together are enough for up to five expedited judgments—if we need that many. One of the guilty parties is still comatose in sick bay, along with two of the people Coby can clear. I'd like to gather up the rest of the squad, charge the guilty and shake down the rest for corroboration for or against the guilt of the last two. Does that meet with your approval?"

"Provisionally, yes. You're keeping Coby here?"

"For his own safety, yes. Until I know whether the duty officer was incompetent or involved. One of the others may have that answer too."

They hashed out a battle plan, and then Marcia left the captain to file paperwork while she finished her due diligence for Public Safety. Her team had inspected the brig and sick bay to confirm that the rest of the squad was being handled properly. All was well on that front. When she got back from her inspection of the unit, she found Captain Jefferson still mired on the paperwork required to document the prisoner interviews. She settled in with her Battalion correspondence to wait for him to finish.

Lights came up in the neighboring interview room again some time later. Jefferson grimaced when the glare slanted over his desk. "Another wellness check already? Sorry, ma'am. I want these reports to be airtight."

"Take your time." Marcia set aside her work and went to the window. "I'm not bored."

A corpsman with delicate purple fur closed the hatch to the interview room with her prehensile tail. She smiled at Corporal Coby as she approached his corner with a medical kit and a pitcher on a tray, but her back-slanted ears and flared ruff were signs of displeasure she couldn't control as easily. Treatment for an injured T-series soldier was menial, not medical. Cleaning and feeding armor-skinned giants who occasionally went berserk was no one's favorite job.

She looked like a toddler next to the corporal's seated bulk, and she held out the pitcher at arm's length. Coby docilely swallowed down whatever was inside. Blood slicked down his chin when he thanked the corpsman afterwards, and his fangs flashed.

The corpsman bounced into full retreat with her tail puffed out.

The missing teeth in Coby's grin gave it an impish quality. He held out the empty pitcher like a sacrificial offering, and when he laughed, the corpsman came stomping back, scolding him about startling her the whole time.

She shook the pitcher threateningly at Coby before setting it aside, and then melted into giggles when he cowered dramatically back. Then she insisted on giving Coby's healing mouth a thorough cleaning, which reminded Marcia of nature documentaries about crocodiles and their attendant birds. The oral hygiene session segued into a full check of all injuries listed on the corporal's chart, and that ended with a pat on Coby's shoulder.

The corpsman walked out of the room wearing a smile, and Marcia looked back at Jefferson. "He's a charmer. It isn't easy to make people comfortable when you look like a fairy-tale monster. Most Tee's give up trying."

"He doesn't know how to give up. He's also smart, and he's better educated than his platoon leader thinks he needs to be." Jefferson paused. "Speaking of Lieutenant Fontaine—I relieved him Monday, pending charges. He didn't review a single promotion or transfer request in the last year. Thankfully, he was also lazy enough that he never deleted any of them. They were all sitting unread in folders."

Marcia counted to ten several times. The past could not be changed. Gateway Company was in Jefferson's good hands now. "Did I miss a question?"

"No. That's background. Coby should be a sergeant. He tested for it, top scores, and he has a strong recommendation from Gunny Rivera. I filed his papers to Battalion HR as soon as I found them in Fontaine's workstation, and HR promptly rejected them. Can you do something about that?"

"Not without a good excuse. HR's decision-making balances a lot of criteria."

"In this case, the sole criterion appears to be saving the Battalion some money," Jefferson said. "Major Ito all but accused me of padding Coby's death benefits."

"Excuse me?"

The captain spread his hands as if offering up his explanation. "Corporal Coby is already years past the typical age for early onset burnout. If he makes it to Labor Day, he'll break the old age record."

Marcia winced inside and allowed herself to shake her head in sympathy. "Then they should be rushing the promotion, not rejecting it. There's a reason Ito's staff call him Major Veto, but I'll have a word."

"Thank you, ma'am." Jefferson nodded at his workstation. "This is done. I've sliced the Gordian knot of red tape. All the indictments and transfers to DPS custody are squared away. We can proceed with filing charges and interviews any time. Ready to light some fires under a few asses?"

He meant it as a joke. It wasn't funny.

"I am ready to incinerate someone." Marcia waved the hatch open and gestured for Jefferson to go first. The captain twitched when the door moved by itself, and when he reached the cool air in the hallway, he gave Marcia a worried glance.

The temperature in the corridor rose several degrees when she reached it. "I hold DPS general ruling powers, remember?" she said. "You command Gateway, but today I'm its judge, jury and executioner all rolled into one. Let's go talk to the real monsters."

BRIG SPECIAL HOLDING WING
20:05S 11 MAY

Marcia was happy to let the captain stew in silence all the way to the T-series holding area. The reinforced corridor walls and the riveted metal hatches were reminiscent of a ship's fittings, except for the sheer size of them. The sound of their footsteps bounced up to 14-foot ceilings.

She relented once they were past the control room and the sergeant-at-arms. "You can relax, Captain. We'll only be questioning your prisoners today, not killing them."

"I was never in doubt, ma'am. If you wanted to char-broil someone, you would order me to invite the whole company to the barbecue. Rules for Courts Martial 806 guarantees speedy, public trial. Even trials by fire."

Marcia stopped dead and wrestled with annoyance. Jefferson hadn't been worried. He'd been dreaming up more bad pyro jokes.

Jefferson stopped too, and lifted eyebrows over a smile. Marcia regarded that innocent face, then leaned closer until sweat broke out on Jefferson's forehead from the radiant heat. "Your sense of humor is treading very close to insubordination, Captain. Do not push me."

His eyes widened. "Wouldn't dream of it, ma'am, not without asbestos gloves."

The assurance was delivered with earnest sincerity, and the audacity of it blew away Marcia's foul temper like a breeze clearing smoke. She chuckled in spite of herself, and the answering twinkle in Jefferson's eyes was her reward.

Sometimes joking in the face of horror was the only way to stay sane. They'd both needed that laugh.

"Does anything rattle you?" Marcia asked as she resumed walking.

"Moths give me the willies." Jefferson fell into step beside her. "And I shrieked like a baby the first time my office assistant here brought me coffee."

"Why? Does she have moth wings?"

"No, she's a precision teleporter. W1. My first day in, still jet-lagged, I start on the admin backlog, and out of nowhere, a mug hits my hand. I hit the ceiling. She hit the floor groveling. It seems that Captain Jordan terrorized everyone he didn't ignore. We're shaking down, but it's been a long month."

In other words, this might not be the last blowup. "You aren't on a desert island, Captain. Draw on Battalion psych support staff at your discretion, and arrange transfers for those who can't be rehabilitated without a fresh start."

"Yesterday, I would've said that wasn't necessary. Today I'll say, 'thank you, ma'am,' and be grateful."

The sentries dogged the hatch behind them, and Marcia's two civilian guards stepped aside. Ginny Ha was an R3, by far the more dangerous of the pair, but at barely five feet tall, wrinkled and smiling, she looked like the doting grandmother she was, when she was off the clock.

Greg Finch was the more visible threat. The badge on his gray DPS uniform marked him as a P2, only one power ranking below Marcia in the same series, and the glow in his pale eyes was an unmistakable warning to those with the sight to see it.

Marcia hoped their powers went untested today. Sustained fire damage and confinement in solid rock were among the few effective ways to subdue a Tee, but both methods were hell on building budgets.

The room normally functioned as a mess hall. Six prisoners in blue brig jumpsuits waited on a row of stools along the cafeteria line. Jefferson halted beside and slightly behind Marcia at the front of the room. "Prisoners! At-ten-SHUN!"

The Marines snapped to their feet. The floor shook underfoot. All of them had the hardened skin, thick muscles, and heavy bones that defined their series designation. Those shared traits erased secondary sexual characteristics, although Marcia knew two were male and four female.

The scientists originally responsible for labeling rollover classes hadn't been compassionate men. T stood for troll.

Marcia matched faces to the records she'd reviewed. Lance Corporal Amy Goodall was a T1A, twelve feet tall from skull to toes. Her armored skin was a dull gold, and so were her dorsal spikes. The broken bones and facial gashes on her medical report from the previous night were fully healed.

The two T3's beside Goodall lacked her height and spines, but they were just as heavily armored. Their claws put Goodall's to shame, and one of them had the huge drooping ears of a B variant.

The last three were all mid-weight T5's, two men with the longer snouts of W variants, and a woman who was re-growing two fingers on her left hand.

They'd all left behind families and careers when onset hit, when their bodies twisted and changed. Goodall had been a professional dancer, T3A Horton, a bank teller, and T3B Lopez, a cook. T5W Smith was a successful entrepreneur and local politician, T5W Bannon, a janitor. T5A Finley taught high school. Ordinary people, from all walks of life.

Marcia said, "The charges are rape and attempted murder. Those are capital offenses under federal statutes for rollovers in your classifications. Some of you are innocent, some are guilty. We're here to cull the goats from the sheep."

"This is bullshit," Smith said. "It was a rampage misfire. They told us rampage accidents don't legally count against us, not while we're in the Corps. If anyone's guilty, it's Coby. He set us off. He admitted it."

Marcia had expected him to protest, and she wasn't surprised that he'd missed the point. "Be silent. Your testimony isn't needed. Your guilt is is incontestable."

"Guilty? Of what? You can't judge us. We didn't do anything wrong. And I have a right to free speech. I have a right to face my accusers. Or—is this about what happened before the rampage? That's bullshit too. That was consensual. If anybody says otherwise, they're lying."

Marcia lost her patience and flicked a glance at Ginny, who nodded.

The floor around Smith's feet bubbled and flowed up his legs to his waist. Once he was secured, Marcia enforced her order. Smith's eyes went wide, and a whisper of sound emerged from his mouth along with the trickle of smoke.

Marcia leaned in, up close and personal. The air rippled with heat.

"I am not here to listen to your excuses," she told him. "I'm here to talk to Marines. Your rights were forfeit the instant your witnessed actions were F-verified. Your reboot camp instructors drilled you in military law and public safety legislation. You cannot claim ignorance, and the Corps does not tolerate barbarism. You are my meat, Smith. The DPS will see you punished for your crime."

She'd wondered, when she reviewed Smith's records jacket, why a man with his education and background wasn't tracked into officer training. The answer was that he'd failed the psych review. Rebooting in the ranks had been his second chance.

Some people never learned. Marcia hoped the rest of the squad understood the lesson she was about to give them. They were all eyeing her with impassive faces and perfectly motionless bodies. "The rest of you—now we see if any of you are still Marines or if you're all barbarians."

She delivered her next command with forceful calm: "*Sit.*"

The Tees dropped to their stools. Their faces remained blank, but their eyes were wary. They'd heard the heat of disgust in her voice.

She let her tone cool again. "But what does that mean, to be a Marine? Captain, you like telling stories. Tell us why you joined the Corps."

"Tradition," Jefferson said promptly. "My screening test came back positive, and my granddad and I had a long talk. My family runs to bangers and carnies, and our R-positives have a sixty-percent rollover rate. Make a virtue of necessity, he said. Pick up a deferred commission with college, get some life experience and come back as a Mercury officer when I hit onset."

For a decade after the first wave of rollovers, the world had lived in fearful ignorance, never knowing who might roll over, or when. A diagnostic blood test screening for onset risk had been one of the Department of Public Safety's first triumphs and remained its greatest achievement.

Today children learned the facts of life in middle school, and every adult who tested positive submitted to an annual exam to track their progress.

Mysteries still outnumbered certainties. Nearly a third of the population carried the blood marker, but relatively few rolled over. Despite a tendency for changes to run in families, a clear genetic link remained elusive.

The biggest enigmas of all were the abilities themselves. Many of the changes that manifested at rollover were simply inexplicable.

Vast amounts of research had been devoted to analyzing phenomena that defied all known laws of biology, chemistry and physics. No one had come up with a working theory to explain them. A lot of studies focused on the tiny, tragic minority who hit onset early in adolescence and usually died before they reached age twenty. The search for a cure, and the search for answers, were both ongoing.

Two points were firmly established: most rollovers occurred between age forty and fifty-five, and the concentration of the blood factor jumped shortly before onset. Those two facts helped people plan for the worst while they hoped for the best, as Jefferson had done.

"But you didn't roll." Marcia said now. "You're a null."

"No, ma'am, I am not. My R-factor spiked through the roof, and I spent a year under DPS evaluation. I'm a Z0Z. Zero on every known power and variance table."

Zeros were rarest of the rare. Most often, onset brought minor modifications. People grew or shrank or changed color, developed minimal psychic talents, or gained an affinity for elements, plants, or animals.

Even those slight alterations could lead to major trauma

and collateral damage, and training the civilian rollover population was the primary mission of the DPS.

Some new abilities were too hazardous for that system to handle. Those who developed dangerous powers were passed to experts in destruction for further education. When an unguarded touch could start deadly epidemics, when one slip of concentration might destroy buildings—or cities—onset was matter of more than one life or death.

They came to Mercury Battalion to be trained in the disciplines needed to put their powers to good use, and after the initial period of adjustment, most returned to their interrupted lives.

Powerless, Jefferson could've immediately gone back to his office, his students, his home. He had not done so.

Marcia asked, "Why not ask for release from your obligation, Captain? I'm sure the appeal would've been granted."

"I signed the contract. Being a Marine isn't about muscle or firepower. It's about honoring the oath."

That was exactly what he'd said the first time they'd had this conversation. Marcia regarded her listening audience. The reminder had sunk in. They were as softened up as they were going to get.

She asked, "Do you see any other Marines here, Captain? If so, they're yours to address."

Jefferson stepped up. "I see Bannon. I see Goodall."

They jumped to their feet.

"Silence is not golden," Jefferson said. "It's criminal. Be witnesses, not accessories. So far, you only face brig time for property damage. Tell us exactly what happened last night, and it ends there."

Marcia said, "Let's make it even easier for you. Here's what we know already." She approached Smith and bared her teeth at him. "This arrogant fuck left his DNA in Stanislav, and witness testimony has been court-verified. His ass is mine."

She walked over to the woman with the missing fingers. "You left trace all over Coby's clothes, and he left teeth in you and Cooper before you pulled him down. You face the same charges the men do, sweetie. Rape is rape. Plus accessory charges, since someone had to unlock that dorm room door in the first place."

The woman lashed out with all eight remaining claws, but Ginny was faster. The concrete was up to Finley's nose before she stopped fighting.

Marcia gave the last two seated prisoners a glare. "Here's all we need to know: where were these two? Stanislav is still unconscious, and Finley hit Coby across the face first. He couldn't see through the blood. Which is it, Marines? Are they guilty or innocent?"

Lopez's big ears went back. Horton dropped to her knees and started sobbing. "I didn't do anything. I didn't know what to do, I didn't—"

"Horton's innocent, ma'am." PFC Bannon said in a rolling basso voice. "She was hiding under her rack when I came in...and...that's all I remember. Sorry, Sue."

Lopez's eyes darted to Goodall, and her claws flexed. "Amy, please."

The lance corporal said softly, "Innocent, sir. What else do you want to know? Coby said be quiet, and I wanted to do right by him, but if he's talked...well. Most of it's pretty clear in my head. I was riding the edge until the very end."

Soon enough, all the new testimony was verified on record, and the worst was over. The four Marine prisoners were returned to their cells. Ginny and Finch took the condemned away to be prepared for transport.

Marcia climbed onto one of the tables and leaned back on her elbows, glad that she'd chosen trousers when the call came in that morning. She stretched out her legs and crossed them at the ankles, wiggling her toes in her shoes. A stiff drink would be nice, but a few moments of undignified relaxation would have to suffice. As long as she got *some* respite from being the hard, unfeeling face of authority.

"You can go, Captain," she said. "I'll oversee the rest of it."

Jefferson hopped onto the neighboring table and swung his legs like a child. "My base, my brig. That wasn't a dismissal from my commander. That was a suggestion from my DPS rep. Where are you taking the prisoners?"

Marcia closed her eyes to keep the pain from showing. "They have to die, Captain. What does it matter how or where? They don't deserve your pity."

There had to be strict limits, because leniency would lead to chaos. Power corrupted unless it was contained. The process held no room for mercy, even if many of those who went astray might never have transgressed if onset hadn't put temptation in their path, if resentment and loss hadn't driven them to actions they once would have considered unthinkable. No villain was ever born evil.

Jefferson remained silent.

Marcia opened her eyes. The captain looked disappointed. Very disappointed. Aggressively disappointed, even. He said, "It isn't pity. They deserve to be drummed out and imprisoned or maybe even executed, but that crack I made about public trials? I meant it. They're human beings. Secrecy poisons justice."

"True enough." DPS summary powers did tread along the thin edge between letter and spirit when it came to the rule of law. That edge was a sharp and uncomfortable place to live.

It wasn't a good system, but it was the only one they had. Marcia put up with the ugliness because she'd seen failure lead to worse tragedy, but she wasn't blind to the harshness.

There were ways to cushion the fall when the hammer of justice came down. Those secrets, unfortunately, were classified far above the captain's pay grade. On the other hand, if she didn't tell Jefferson the truth, she risked losing his trust for good. That would be a terrible waste.

"They die," she said. "That's as much of the story as I can tell. I can share some historical trivia, though."

Jefferson searched her face, and his scowl lightened. "Is that so? I do like random facts. Go on, please."

"After WWII, the US claimed sovereignty over hundreds of tiny islands, scattered over thousands of square miles of ocean. They're uninhabitable, even if people wanted to be that close to the China Wall. No reliable fresh water, no shelter from typhoons, no food except what the sea and palms provide. It's quite a shame. They're beautiful, in a remote, isolated way. I've seen several of them."

"Have you, now? Interesting." Jefferson slid to the floor and made a show of straightening his uniform before heading for the exit. "If the Wall comes down, those islands will be the front lines of any containment efforts. Too bad they can't be used as surveillance outposts."

"Very sad."

Survival on those atolls and cays occasionally required superhuman strength and endurance, but someone with those traits and a few basic supplies could live in reasonable comfort. The DPS didn't abandon its exiles. Some of them even earned the right to come home again. Not many, but a few.

There were other havens for the condemned with other

powers, other parts of the world that needed watching, places where the DPS and the Corps offered their dead a second chance, or even a third one, to atone for their sins.

Jefferson paused at the hatch. "Good night, Colonel. Thank you for the story."

"You're welcome, Captain. Good job, today. Let's never do this again."

"I'll do my best, ma'am."

He would, and it wouldn't be enough. It never was. Sometimes rules were all that kept civilization going, but the harsh necessities were too much for some to bear, and tragedies like this one would keep happening. If Marcia never had to strip the last hope of a normal life from a flawed human as the price for failure, it would be too soon.

Her reverie ended when she realized Jefferson was still waiting. When she met his eyes, he said, "One last thing, Colonel. With your permission."

That was seldom a good sign. Marcia tensed. "Go ahead, Captain."

"I just wanted to say I'm glad we're developing a decent working relationship." He paused. "Would it be fair to say you're starting to warm up to me?"

Marcia's shoulder muscles loosened. She said stiffly, "Good *night*, Captain Jefferson."

He shut the hatch behind him, which meant Marcia could laugh as long and as hard as she wanted without damaging her image.

And if the laughter turned to cleansing tears in due time, well then. She was alone, and her feelings were her own.

MIDNIGHT CALL

DEPARTMENT OF PUBLIC SAFETY INCIDENT RECORD
94156-B14-2015

17 OCTOBER, 23:56 CALL ANOMALY FLAGGED

BEGIN TRANSCRIPT

OPERATOR: Hello, you've reached Crossroads
    Support Center. How can we help you?
FEMALE CALLER: Hello, hi, this the rollover hotline,
    isn't it? Can I talk to someone? Do I have to say who
    I am?
O: No, you don't have to identify yourself. You can talk
    to me, your privacy is protected. How can we help?
    Crossroads specializes in all aspects of onset. I'm
    Eileen. Ask me anything.
C: I think I'm going to die. (crying in background) I'm
    so scared.
O: Being frightened is normal, but hundreds of people

go through rollover every year. A positive test result isn't the end of your life. What's worrying you? Employment leave? Finances? We can help you file for legal protection and hardship grants. Do you have children? Are you married? We offer counseling for that.

(15 seconds silence)

O: Are you still with me? Don't be scared. We can help. It's what we do.

C: I'm thirteen.

O: I'm so sorry, I didn't catch that. You said thirty?

C: No, thirteen. I'm thirteen.

O: Oh.

C: I know, right? I'm going to die, aren't I? Everybody knows that if the change hits when you're still a kid then you die. I only got my period last year. I don't want to die. Why is this happening? Why? (crying)

O: Oh, baby, please stay on the line. Hang on. I need...

(background mumbling)

C: Hello?

O: Sorry, honey. I'm listening. I have to ask this. Are you sure? You haven't even had your first official blood screening. Are you absolutely sure it's onset?

C: Yes, I'm sure! I am not being hysterical. Mom always tells me I'm being dramatic, but I'm not. I took Advanced Health this year, and I got 100% on the Rollover Symptoms unit.

O: That's good. That's great. You sound like a smart

girl. I'm trying to make sure I get the details right. Tell me your symptoms. Can you do that?

C: There was a spot on my arm today when I was dressing after gym, all blue and sparkly, and it didn't come off even when I scrubbed. I was late to English and everybody stared at me. I think they know.

O: Let's not focus on that. Could it be a bruise?

C: You don't believe me, do you? I know what bruises look like. (rustling) It's bigger now, all down my side, and it itches. I don't want to roll over. I'm going to die, and I'll hurt other people first if I'm a banger or a plague rat, and you don't even believe me. I don't know why I even bothered calling. I should go.

O: Wait, please. Don't end the call. I do believe you, I promise. Stay on the line with me. Tell me how you're feeling.

C: I'm hot. Do you know what's sad? I haven't even had a real kiss yet. Only a stupid spin-the-bottle kiss with Lee at Bethany's birthday party last summer, and one with Frank after homeroom. Were those sins? Is that why this is happening? I try to be good, I truly do.

(background mumbling)

O: I'm sure you are a very good girl. You're smart, calm, and very helpful. Help me understand. Keep talking. Why are you thinking about sins?

18 OCTOBER 00:02
DEPARTMENT OF PUBLIC SAFETY NATIONWIDE
ALERT ISSUED, ASSIGNMENT PENDING
TARGET.

C: Is this happening because I'm a sinner? Is it God's
    punishment? It's so hard to be good. I peeked at the
    back of the math book on the assignment, and that
    was a sin too, wasn't it? This all my fault because
    I'm lustful and a cheater.
O: Oh, God. No, baby. No. It's biology, not
    punishment. You said the spot on your arm was
    shimmery. Tell me more about that.
C: It was more of a glow than a shimmer. I'm glowing
    all over now. I feel so *hot*. I'm going to be a banger,
    aren't I? I'm going turn into a torch or a cherry
    bomb or worse, and I thought so, that's why I made
    Celine cry at dinner, so she would sleep with Mom
    and Dad instead of in here with me, but...oh, I'm so
    sorry. God will hear me if I say I'm sorry, won't he?
    If I promise I will never be bad again, will this stop?
O: Oh, you poor thing.

        (Muttering. Inaudible conversation)

18 OCTOBER 00:05
CROSSROADS PHONE TRACE PLACES TARGET AT
<ADDRESS REDACTED>

DEPARTMENT OF PUBLIC SAFETY UNIT 216
AND MERCURY BATTALION HEAVY RESPONSE
TEAM SCRAMBLED. STANDARD NOTIFICATION
SENT TO LOCAL AUTHORITIES.

O: Baby, listen. Help is on its way. You don't have to be scared. Everything will be all right now.

C: Help? Help from where? How do they know where I am? You told! You said you wouldn't, but you told on me, didn't you? I trusted you!

O: Yes, you did, and I'm doing the best I can for you. Please don't be angry at me. Don't hang up. I'm sorry I had to tell other people, but you said your parents are there, and your sister. Think about them. You're a good girl, and you want to do the right thing. You don't want anyone to get hurt, right?

C: No, of course I don't want to hurt anyone, but I don't want go away, either. Oh, I wish—

(5 seconds silence)

O: Are you still there?

(12 seconds silence)

O: Baby? Can you talk to me?

C: It's for the best, isn't it? (crying) I don't want to hurt Mom or Dad, not even when I get mad and say I hate everybody. When they come to take me away, it's for the best, but I'm so scared. Will they hurt me?

O: No, baby, I promise they only want to help, to keep you safe, and your family, and everyone.

C: I'm supposed to forgive people when they sin against me. I have to forgive you, don't I? I do. I forgive you for telling on me.

O: (throat clearing) You *are* a good girl. Thank you. How are you feeling now?

C: My sheets smell funny. They're turning all dark. I think they're burning, only really slowly. I *don't* understand why this had to happen. I don't drink or do drugs or stay out late, I turn in my assignments, I only cheated once ever. Maybe twice. Those aren't sins that would make God this angry, are they? Why is God doing this to me?

O: I wish I knew, baby. Help is coming. Stay right where you are.

C: I will. They won't blame me, will they? This isn't my fault. It isn't fair. I try so hard to be good.

O: Yes, you are. You are good. It's no one's fault. Try not to be angry, sweetie. Stay calm.

C: They'll come for me soon, won't they?

O: Yes, baby. They'll be there soon. I'll stay with you on the phone. I'm here, baby. I won't leave you. You aren't alone. Just keep holding on.

C: Oh. Oh, no. I'm so sorry, but the glow—I tried—

(static)
(connection lost)

END TRANSCRIPT

18 OCTOBER 01:17 INITIAL INCIDENT DATA
Containment: successful
Fatalities: 0 Injuries: 3 Property loss: total
Preliminary assessment: Pyrokinetic Rank 1, variant C

18 OCTOBER 02:15 TRANSFER SUMMARY

Mercury Command cedes incident control to Public Safety
Unit 216. Target transferred to DPS supervision for initial
Adaptation processing. Custodial rights successfully transferred to the Department without parental challenge. Subject
transported immediately to DPS Camp Garfield for full evaluation and training pending Mercury Battalion intake.

END INCIDENT REPORT

*FILE NOTATION: Personal details redacted per Civilian Privacy
Act 45 CFR 5b*

NIGHTMARE

OWL'S NEST SALOON, ELGIN ILLINOIS

ALL EYES in the bar turned to Kris the instant she ducked inside the front door. Music with a thumping bass beat assaulted her ears, a flood of new scents washed over her with the shift in air pressure, and blinking lights dazzled her. Every muscle went tight, and fear buzzed along her nerves. Power surged though her flesh, pooling in the muscles, thickening her skin.

Her pacifier necklace beeped a sullen warning, responding to the pheromone release that accompanied the power flare. Then the chilly metal circlet vibrated a secondary alert, and needles emerged to prick her skin. She put one hand to her throat and struggled to calm herself. The device could penetrate her normal armoring, and her skin would never harden further while she was wearing the pacifier. The sedative would drop her before she could shift.

This did not look like a safe place to pass out. Most of the patrons were big-bellied, broad-shouldered men in plaid and denim. A few were partnered with women in plaid tops and short skirts. Ten gallon hats and feed caps went head to head with bandanas in a battle for hair-coverage supremacy, and frowns were the universal choice of expression.

A young woman behind the bar at the back of the room called out, "Hi, beautiful! You must be here for the party. C'mon over, grab some pitchers for your buddies."

The sound of a friendly voice, female and cheerful, tipped Kris off the nervous edge of panic towards calm. She took a deep, cleansing breath, the way she'd been taught in therapy. The odors of stale beer and stale bodies filled her nose, but the familiar routine did the trick. Her nerves settled, the pacifier fell silent, and she dredged up the courage to move forward.

A promise was a promise. She couldn't say *no* to a birthday girl, even if Amy was turning fifty-five. Besides, she couldn't hide on base forever. She had at least thirty months left in her hitch.

The crowd silently stared as Kris passed by. She kept an eye on the light fixtures. She'd cleared ten feet before her rollover ended in a T-series designation and compulsory military training. The height came with metallic armored skin and massive musculature that still felt strange almost a year after the first changes hit. For this occasion, she wore the one tailored civilian outfit she owned, but she knew the clothes only accentuated her strangeness.

No one looking at her would guess that she'd suckled two children at her breasts, or that her hips had passed them into the world. The breasts were as flat as a boy's, the pelvis so altered that learning to walk properly had taken weeks of practice. The other patrons were staring at the monster Kris saw when she looked in a mirror.

She tried to avoid mirrors. The one on the wall behind the bottles at the bar taunted her with glimpses of short black hair, shiny bronze skin and gold eyes full of worry. That was her new face. The red silky shirt below it hung loose on her chest. Some of the faces reflected behind her looked more than shocked. They looked hateful, and Kris wished she could sink through the floor and disappear.

The bartender said to the room at large, "Shut yer mouths before flies git in, people. Never seen a Marine before?"

The tension broke with an intangible pop. People started talking again. Billiard balls hit one another with clacking sounds. Glasses and bottles clinked.

"Thanks for that," Kris said to the bartender.

"You're here for Corporal Goodall's birthday, yeah? Here ya go. This is her favorite, and James doesn't have it on tap back there." She slid two pitchers of frothy amber liquid across the bar and pointed to a closed door near a hall marked RESTROOMS & PHONES. "That's our accommodation zone. We've a big door around the side, too, if you want to go direct next time. Most of the grunts do."

Kris glanced into the mirror again, caught sight of unfriendly eyes looking away fast. "I can see why. I'd say sorry, but—" But she wasn't sorry. Angry, embarrassed, helpless and frustrated, all that, but not sorry.

The woman's lips twisted in a wry smile. "No worries, honey. You're welcome in my place any time. I've got a cousin out west with Empire Company. Eyes front, now. Forward, march."

Inside the door, Kris went down steps to a sunken floor that brought the ceiling to sixteen feet high. Seats tailored to inhuman forms were the norm here: tables sat on a platform around the perimeter, equipped with chairs in all sizes, including backless stools for the winged and tailed. A concrete dance floor was the centerpiece, and hammocks for those who preferred perches to seats swung overhead in the corners. This room was as crowded as the front one. Many of the occupants looked just as human too, but fur and feathers were common, and Kris wasn't the only rare T-series present. Amy was on the dance floor, and it looked like half the base had come out to cheer her on.

A second bar stood next to the door, tended by a long-limbed man who had a black chitinous exoskeleton and feathery antennae. Kris lifted the pitchers. "Where do I take these? For Amy Goodall."

"For you, too." He hung a mug off her pinkie finger and pointed at an unoccupied cluster of tables at the back. "Up there, honey."

Kris maneuvered through the spectators lining the dance square and cleared a spot for the beer amidst a cluster of half-empty glasses. Then she sat down to watch the birthday girl work up a thirst.

Amy was a sight to behold as she danced solo across the empty floor. Twelve feet tall, gold and leathery from top to toe, she was dressed in a glitter-gold halter top and a short swirling skirt. Her dorsal spines went from nubs at her waist to a tall crest atop her skull. Fuzzy black hair surrounded the pair of gleaming polished horns that curved down to defend her cheekbones. Her eyes were warm gold, and her face was rapt with happiness.

She pirouetted once, twice, and a third time, then began a series of soaring leaps that took her around and around the floor. The maneuver ended with a bound to the center, where she came down hard enough to shake the walls. Just as the song ended, she struck a pose: back arched, one leg stretched behind, hands overhead, claws extended. The audience cheered, and a new song began. Amy left the floor with a laugh and a bow, and eager dancers quickly filled the space.

Amy pulled a stool up to the table and lifted lips over pointed teeth. "Hey, Stan! What'd you think? Be honest. You can tell me I look like a hippo in a tutu. Tonight, I don't care. it's my birthday, and I'll dance if I want to."

You were breathtaking, like a dragon in flight. That was what Kris wanted to say, but Amy's words put a lump of emotion in her throat. Her last name was Stanislav, but she hadn't heard the shortened version since she transferred.

She'd hated her first squad leader for saddling her with the manly nickname, but coming from Amy now, it was a reminder of happier days. In her new unit she was called by rank, her full name, or nothing. Mostly nothing. Her fingers rose to fiddle with the pacifier, and she swallowed memories both good and bad.

"You make our ugliness beautiful when you move," she said.

"Ha. I knew I could count on you for honest flattery." Amy poured them each a drink. "I love being able to do leaps like that again. Here's to having brand-new knees I can't ruin—" Her eyes fell to Kris's collar, and she froze mid-toast. "Shit on a stick. I forgot you were still restricted, from the—you know, that night. How are you doing, Stan? I've barely seen your grumpy face since the transfer."

That night, she called it. Kris closed her eyes as memory made her gasp for breath that wouldn't come. She fought for air against fingers pressing her lips so hard against her own teeth that the flesh tore and bled, her shoulder popped out of joint with an crunch of bone and sinew, and all around there was raucous laughter—

Her heart pounded. She couldn't blame Amy for avoiding the word rape. She didn't want to use it either, or think about it, or remember it. Too bad she didn't have the choice. *She kicked, but her feet were caught and held, and she pedaled furiously against air, twisting her body without moving it at all. Her legs were pulled apart, and weight slammed down on her, into her—*

She stepped back inside her head the way her therapist had taught her, and the memory eased. The pacifier stayed quiet, and she said with pride, "I re-test for active duty in a week. I'm going to pass." During the first few weeks she'd needed the thing to prevent her from wreaking havoc every time she flashed into a panic. Now it was an annoyance. She'd been automatically assigned to a new squad, no one talked about *that night*, and life went on. It wasn't easy, but it was all she could do.

"Of course you'll pass. You're tough as nails and smart as a — shit." Amy's eyes went wide. "I just realized. You came in through the bar, didn't you?"

"Yes. I didn't know there was a back door." Kris pushed away her mug as her stomach lurched with worry. "Why?"

"A few local assholes love this place too much to leave it to monsters and monster lovers. We try to keep anyone on restricted duty out of their sight. Fuck."

"I'm sorry." She was always doing something wrong. Why hadn't she screamed for help that night? Why hadn't she fought harder? "I didn't mean to cause trouble."

"Nah, I should've warned you." Amy stood up. "Sarge! Up here!"

The music was loud. Amy was louder. One of the few other Tees in the room turned around, and when Kris saw his face, she wanted to either die on the spot or kill Amy. Maybe both. Sergeant Jack Coby was the last person on the planet she ever wanted to see again, here or anywhere.

"You invited him?" she asked. "If you'd told me he was here, I would've stayed home.

"That's why I didn't tell you," Amy said. "It's also a bar, Stan. Kind of public. Hush, now. I want his help."

"Whassup, Goodie?" Sergeant Coby asked as he came up the steps. His voice was an emotionless bass drone, and reflective glasses hid his expression. He made Kris's skin crawl with nervousness, even though she had two feet of height on him. He might be so thin-skinned that the plating didn't show unless he went into rampage, but he had an air of authority even when he was swaying on his feet.

He nodded at Kris. "Stan. Good'ta seeya out an' about."

Amy said, "You are drunk, Sergeant Jackass."

He grinned. "I am. Is'sa party, righ'? So, whassup?"

Amy pointed at the pacifier. "That. The barflies saw it, and you know how they get about ambushing ironheads. Can we get a PSA?"

"Sure can." Coby broke into another toothy grin and swung to face the crowd. "Attention on deck, Marines!" His basso shout made Amy's earlier yell sound like a whisper. Someone cut the music, and he continued, "Word is, we might have to fight our way home tonight. How do you feel about that?"

A cheer went up, and Jack laughed. "Mission objective: everyone hauling iron gets home vertical. Buddy up. Rules of engagement: no biting, no cocoons, no poisons, no transformations, no illusions. Start nothing, safety first. Got it?"

"Aw, Sarge," someone said plaintively, and laughter rose. "There," Jack said to Amy. "S'all good. Happy fucking birthday."

He wobbled back to the dance floor. The music started up again. Kris swallowed hard. "I didn't think we could get drunk," she said.

"It takes work. Swallow a bottle of cough syrup, toss back a handful of allergy pills, and stick to 180 proof shit. Jackass is becoming an artist at it." Amy filled her own glass and nudged Kris's mug with the pitcher. "I'd rather enjoy all the beer I can afford without powering up to burn it off."

Then she raised her glass. "Happy fucking birthday to me, happy fucking night out for you. Happy fucking anti-hang-over rampage for Sarge."

Kris took a sip of the beer. It was bitter and bubbly, a lot like her feelings about Coby. "I don't grasp why boys love booze so much. Little Matt drinks himself sick with his frat brothers every weekend and leaves me slobbery messages. The therapist says he does it to relieve stress. I guess that makes sense. All these changes have been hard on him."

"Right, and it's been so easy for you." Amy sighed. "I don't know how you do this with a family, Stan. Me, I'm starting to love this life—turns out unarmed combat is a lot like dancing —but I didn't even have a dog to leave behind. You, though— well. What a nightmare. How is Big Matt handling things these days?"

"I got my Dear Jane papers yesterday." Confessing the pain was easier than Kris expected. "I signed. I'm officially divorced."

Amy rubbed at one of her horns in an embarrassed gesture. "Well that's a kick in the ass. Damn, woman."

Guilt stabbed at her. "Sorry to ruin the mood."

"You're joking, right?" Amy took a deep swallow of beer. "It's another reason to celebrate. You're well rid of the asshole.

I met him once, remember? After the—you know. You want to talk about it?"

Kris spoke before she thought. "No, I don't want to talk about it. Do you want to talk about being old enough to get senior discounts? What good will talking do either of us?"

Amy inhaled enough beer to choke herself. Once she stopped coughing and laughing, she said, "Damn, I love it when you use that sassy Mom voice. Drink up. We'll drown our sorrows together.

The second beer tasted better than the first, and Amy kept pouring. People came and went, delivering good wishes, hugs, and more beer, but no one stayed long. Kris relaxed and tried to keep her self-pity in check.

Matheus had cut out her heart and crushed it, but he never meant to do it. She drank to keep her hands occupied and to keep herself from crying. She couldn't wish him ill even now.

Their marriage had been over since the day she'd looked at her new body in a barracks mirror and thought, *well, at least the stretch marks are gone* before bursting into tears.

Her physical relationship with her husband had died the instant she finished her first rollover rampage, standing in the clinic with torn muscles healing under skin as hard as an alligator's back, staring down at tiles that were four feet farther from eye level than they'd been a few minutes earlier.

She'd known her husband would never see her as a desirable woman again, but she believed him when he insisted that they shared more than a bed as man and wife. She'd wanted so much to believe that love did conquer all.

She'd lied to herself until Matheus visited sick bay after *that night*, when his scent betrayed his revulsion even before Kris opened her eyes to see him at her bedside. He flinched when she said his name. That was the beginning of the end.

Turning into a monster hadn't destroyed her marriage. Being raped had done that.

Of all the cruel tricks God had played on Kris, that was the cruelest one. Matheus had been willing to stay married to a monster, but he couldn't love a victim.

The space in her chest where love had lived was an ache that begged to be filled with anger.

She and Amy were working on the fifth pitcher when Amy said, "You know, when you said *boys like him*, earlier, it made me stop and think. I always forget how young Coby is, because he's so damned good. Sergeant Hansen has thirty-five years on him, but he's twice the Marine she is. I hate to say it, her being your new squad leader and all, but she's a fuckin' Gomer. You heard we had to bail her ass out of a literal fire yesterday?"

"Yes. I sat in the office and wrote the incident reports today. Don't be mean." Sergeant Hansen might not be the sharpest knife in the drawer, but she was patient, and she was kind. "Anyone could've made the same mistake. Who would expect a bystander to throw a rolling pyro into a car and drive off?"

"Anyone who can read a mission brief. The family's religious affiliation was on page one, for fuck's sake. Don't defend her, Stan. She went in soft. You're so new you're shiny, and you're already more professional than she'll ever be. What's SOP for a hostile high-risk retrieval, huh? Or don't you remember?"

Plans and puzzles were the fun part of the job. Kris didn't even have to think hard. "Command confirms location. Access teleporters bring in the team. Kickers clear the site, brutes engage, exit porters bungee everyone back to containment."

She frowned at her empty mug. She hadn't practiced that scenario since transferring. Her new unit did not drill, or keep up with procedural developments, or *care* the way Sergeant Coby had made them care.

She'd thought, when she arrived at Camp Butler to join Gateway Company, that all platoons were the same. She'd believed her instructors when they'd said the Corps was about discipline and honor and pride in service. The last couple of months had been an unwelcome lesson about the depths to which reality could sink below the ideal.

Even thinking that felt disloyal. She said, "My solution leaves at least one Tee in sickbay for days with target damage, and it puts two porter teams out of commission for recovery leave too. Can't blame Hansen for trying to minimize Corps casualties."

"Sure I can. We go out there to protect innocents, not avoid losses. If that pyro had hit full ignition five minutes earlier, she could've incinerated five hundred people. You know how to do the right thing. Hansen doesn't. She and her butterbar don't deserve you."

Before rollover, Kris would have blushed at a compliment. She still felt a rush of warmth. It was good to be appreciated. "Well, they have me. I'll make the best of it."

"You get to request assignment after you re-test, you know. Your transfer was bullshit. It's automatic after barracks incidents, but in your case—the rotten assholes were gone, and us girls would've held your hand through the worst of the aftermath, if we'd been allowed. We'd love to have you back. There's a bunk for you in our dorm if you want it."

"I can't." The thought of it sent fear washing over her. Knowing her assailants were dead—execution being the punishment meted out to all violent rollover criminals—that was the only reason she slept at all some nights. "No. I couldn't handle the memories." Specifically, she couldn't handle seeing Jack Coby every day.

"Too bad," Amy said. "Mandatory therapy is not bullshit, but bitch sessions and pedicures help too. Guess I'll have to come and visit your new digs more often."

With that, Amy stood and stretched, yawning. "Things are winding down. You don't go home alone, not with that doggy collar on. You'd be a target for every bigoted redneck in the county. Want to come with me, or wait 'til last call and let Jackass escort you?"

The dance floor was empty, and only a few tables were still occupied. Sergeant Coby and a T-series woman Kris didn't recognize were deep in conversation in a booth. There was no reason to stay, and every reason to leave. "I'll come with you, but I'm warning you now, it won't work."

"What won't?"

"You're going to spend the whole walk trying to talk me into transferring back. It won't work."

Amy grinned. "Smartypants. See why I want you on my team?" They were nearly to the door when the plan fell apart. Two teleporters in uniform appeared back-to-back in the middle of the dance floor.

One was looking straight at Kris.

"Locked," the woman said, and the partner facing the other side of the room said, "Confirm lock." The world turned inside out, and Kris sank knee-deep in snow.

Amy fell on her butt in a drift. "What the actual fuck?" she said, and the porters disappeared.

SOMEWHERE DEFINITELY NOT THE OWL'S NEST
SALOON

A SPHERE of dim red light floated overhead, illuminating a fifty foot circle of snow well enough make out the crates stacked at the center. Kris's breath clouded the air in front of her face, clearing when she took in a lungful of searing cold. Her skin automatically rippled and thickened in response, and she held her breath until she was sure the pacifier would ignore the protective reflex.

Alarm klaxons and sirens wailed in the distance. Lieutenant Akron's voice shouted orders nearby in the dark. The lit circle had the look of a night operation in progress, but that was where familiarity ended. *But I'm off-duty* was Kris's first thought, followed by, *And I'm restricted. And this isn't even my unit any more.*

Confusion was no excuse for inaction. Kris turned to check her six. Sergeant Coby had been scooped up too. All around, porters popped in with passengers and out again. Most of the arrivals were as inappropriately dressed as Kris was. Pinpoints of light flared and disappeared far out in the darkness too: Marines 'porting into perimeter positions. It was definitely a major op of some kind. A lumpy object fell out of nowhere, and she automatically lifted her arms to catch it.

Beside her, Amy cradled her own bundle of boots, harness and weapons. A pale figure who looked like an albino fox in a uniform trotted past in the distant gloom. Amy took a deep breath and bellowed, "LT, what the fuck is going on?"

"Shut up, suit up, and pump up," Lieutenant Akron called back. "Brief in five."

"Aye-aye, sir." Amy shook her head and started dressing.

Kris did the same. She was nearly done when a tingle of power stroked over her, lighting up her nerves and sending the pacifier into conniptions. "Not now," she whispered at it as she buckled up. "That isn't me. Behave, you stupid thing." She did not want to be sedated in the middle of a crisis.

"Sorry, Stan. My bad," Sergeant Coby said behind her. "I wanted to burn off the booze ASAP. Forgot about your collar already, because, y'know, drunk. Hang on."

He moved into view shouting, "Iron on the LZ. I say again, we have iron on the LZ. All Tees clear fifty downwind before pumping up."

He was already rigged for combat: uniform pants, harness and helmet on, eyes bright below the brim of the raised visor. *How did he dress so fast?* Kris wondered.

He carried a melee baton in one hand and a field radio in the other, and leftover energy from his rampage flare wisped off him in a glowing mist. The scutes of his full armoring bulged over bands of augmented muscle.

"You all right?" he asked.

Kris jammed her boots onto her feet with an aggravated stomp. "No, I'm not all right! I shouldn't even be here. I'm restricted, dammit."

Her heart pounded, and the pacifier kept griping away, although it hadn't started its warning vibration. Annoyance was a relatively safe emotion. "What kind of stupid fucking question is that, Sarge? What the actual fuck?"

The equipment harness would not cooperate. She loosened the buckles and muttered another few expletives under her breath. Before rollover, the worst word she'd ever said aloud was darn. Everything had changed since then.

Amy cleared her throat, loudly, and Kris froze. *What am I thinking, sassing a sergeant?*

And Amy said, "I'm stepping aside to pump up, Stanny. Be right back."

Sergeant Coby moved in, and Kris automatically shifted back.

Coby tilted his head back, squinting up at her. "There's a trick to harness when it's this cold. Lift your arms, and I can show you." When Kris hesitated, he added mildly, "Want me to make that an order? Want Goodie to do it instead?"

That was a trap. Either option would be admitting failure. Kris chose the only right answer. She lifted her arms.

Coby tugged at the snagged harness, just so, and everything slid into place over knobby armor and cloth. He backed off, and Kris did up the final buckles. Then she shrugged experimentally to see if she could do the trick herself next time.

She never doubted there would be a next time. Waking up sweating and terrified, knowing she was useless and a coward, bursting into tears for no reason at the strangest moments—when she suited up for work, those troubles disappeared, replaced by purpose and determination. She could do the job. It was too bad and totally not her fault she couldn't do it properly today.

"I can't join formation," she pointed out. "Not with this collar on."

"Not a problem. The iron is coming off," Coby said, turning to survey the area. "Gunny! A hand, here."

Kris tensed. "Coming off? How? Only the psych board has the codes, and I'll get in trou—"

Gunnery Sergeant Rivera arrived before she finished her protest. He was dark-skinned and bald and had no physical variance at all, which meant he looked human in most circumstances and like a midget next to Sergeant Coby.

He leaned way back to look Kris in the eye. "Worried about going on report? Now? Y'might want to rethink your priorities, Marine. I'm authorized for field evals, so bend over. This won't hurt a bit."

It was an order so she obeyed, but she wondered how he could remove the device without setting off the anti-tampering feature.

Rivera could bench-press a whale and cross a football field too fast to be seen, but he wasn't invulnerable. The explosion would knock Kris out. It could blow off the gunny's arms.

He raised his hands and held them at her neck. "Who's doing the honors?" he asked.

"Me," Amy said, striding up. She really looked dragon-like now, with every spike raised in full armor, gold and thick. The LEDs on her custom headset were all lit too, glowing like jewels against her horns. She smiled down at Kris and slipped her fingers under Rivera's hands, around the pacifier. "See what we're up to, smartypants?" she asked.

Kris nodded. "You're going to flare." The activation protocol would give Rivera an instant's leeway to yank it clear before it detonated, and Amy's armor would protect him from the blast. "That will trigger me too, won't it?"

"It will, and it'll hit like a hammer," Amy said. "Ride it and bank the power. You can do it."

The gunny took a firm grip on Amy's wrists. "On my mark. Three, two, one, mark."

It was over so fast Kris didn't even have time to blink. The night flared orange, heat blasted her face—Rivera was laughing—and the screaming power of Amy's rampage hit like a kick to the spine.

Kris bucked and shuddered as the fire in her body sparked awful memories of the last time she'd been pumped up this high. The need to use those pulsing, growing muscles drove out rational thought, demanding she destroy *something* with it.

Her legs cramped with the strain of standing still when she needed to leap and run and hit-hit-hit the whole world.

Then Amy's arms were around her. "Breathe, baby. Suck it in. Suck in the calm, blow out the excess, find the sweet spot."

Kris inhaled Amy's perfume along with all the other scents in the cold air, brought them deep into her chest. Pheromones could damp the internal shifts the same way they could send an uncontrolled rampage roaring through a whole T-series unit like a storm.

She pictured herself balancing in the flow the way her daughter Eryka glided along smooth cold ice on the edge of a skate blade. The energy flowed smooth through her, answering to her will, and she exhaled, whistling.

Rivera brushed debris off his hands and handed Kris her combat helmet. "Not bad for a boot. I like a fast learner."

Amy followed him when he walked away, and Kris fell in behind her. They joined the crowd gathering around the supply drop.

Tents, frames and tech were unboxed, and the command post went up in less than ten minutes. Sergeant Coby huddled up there with Rivera and a Tee wearing sergeant's insignia who Kris didn't know.

She only recognized a dozen people, in fact, and when a short woman went zipping by with a power cable, Kris spotted a unit badge she didn't remember.

She eyed the other personnel—seven Tees, two pyros shimmering with heat on bare patches of ground, a variety pack of carnies whose powers could not be discerned from

their variant bodies, others looking as human as any null—
and then sorted through her mental file of scenarios.

More than a platoon was present, but no squad was repre-
sented in full, and most of them had arrived unprepared. This
was a scratch op, and that meant the whole Battalion was
responding to emergencies. Multiple rollovers or unsanc-
tioned power demonstrations must happening at once.

They were deployed in an attack formation, not the standard envelopment used to contain a hot rollover. All around
there was only snow, more snow and a low, rolling horizon.
The frigid air carried trace odors of old vegetable oil, smoke,
sulfur and metal. The scents told Kris there were paved roads
nearby, and a kitchen large enough to need a commercial
grease trap.

"High-power meltdown at a DPS camp," she said, thinking
aloud. "A new quakemaker or pyro, judging from the number
of Tees here. Where, I wonder? Is this Kansas? Alaska? Is
DPSC Anchorage on flatlands?"

"It's Kansas," Lieutenant Akron said as he passed by. His
tail was flicking in agitation. "You want to run the briefing for
me, lance corporal?"

Kris wanted to sink right into the snow and die. Her body
had other ideas about what to do with the embarrassment.
Her dorsal spines rose and went rigid, and her harness
creaked as scutes shifted and settled.

Amy elbowed her in the ribs. "Down, Marine."

Lieutenant Akron stopped beside Gunny Rivera under the
command post awning. His pointy ears swiveled back and
forth as he looked over the gathered troops.

When he was done making them all wait, he said, "Listen
up, people. Mercury is riding a rollover cluster tonight. Over
a dozen deployments nationwide. Every on-duty unit was

already engaged when a divination tip came in from a fortuneteller in Allegheny. We're stuck punching the hunch ticket on a breakout prevention."

He bared his teeth at the collective groan that met his announcement. "Yes it's possible we're here for nothing, but if the stars align wrong, then a new R1A is about to go natural catastrophe all over DPSC Fort Atkinson. She's a plate-shaker. If the situation develops as predicted, we are tasked to stop her at all costs."

He went over the details of the plan, and Kris was struck by its similarity to the containment scenario she and Amy had discussed at the party. The differences made this a far riskier proposition. Detaining an unwilling intern on the verge of rollover was one thing. Stopping someone who could already express her new talents was another.

If the earthmover did commandeer a departing bus full of visitors in a doomed escape attempt, then she was as good as dead. Even the trapped visitors in the bus would be considered expendable balanced against the population of the state or the eastern half of the country. An earthmover who could interfere with plate tectonics was a threat to millions.

Kris understood the woman's desperation all too well. She wanted to go home too. She wanted to tuck her children into bed, to cook suppers and box up lunches, to return to an everyday life. Some days, her heart ached from wake-up to lights-out, and every glimpse of regular life was a reminder of what she'd lost.

Sympathy would not stand in the way of duty. *Contain, protect, preserve*: that was the motto of Mercury Battalion. Kris had waved good-bye to a camp bus carrying away her children every weekend once she'd finished rollover and earned the right to visitations, before she went to Mercury to star her

real training. In her mind's eye, she saw Eryka's smiling face
pressed against a window, could see her waving back. When
she imagined that bus sinking into a fiery mass of lava, her
heart thumped and her breath shortened.

The earthmover's name was Grace Bell. The lieutenant
added that humanizing touch apologetically, but Kris was
glad to have a name to put into her prayers. Predictions went
wrong. A tiny element changed, and a crisis never happened.
She sent her hopes rising to heaven in silence, and she
followed Amy and Sergeant Coby to their designated ready
point.

They were the reserve. If they went into action, it would
mean dozens were already dead and thousands more were
doomed. If the primary team failed, then she, Amy, and Coby
were charged with pinning down Grace long enough that an
orbital bombardment could be precision-targeted.

Kris had started the night terrified of a bar fight. The
possibility of being pulverized in an artificial meteorite strike
before dawn really put things in perspective.

She prayed for Eryka and Matty, and even for Matheus,
should she die here. Most of all she prayed Grace Bell found
the strength to not break down and start a chain of destruction that might kill them all.

The rest of their team—four porters and an air elemental
—joined them, and Sergeant Coby ran a capabilities-and-
limitations briefing. Then he insisted on role-playing potential scenarios while they waited for orders. Kris appreciated
the effort. Dry runs were no substitute for unit experience,
but studying maps and walking through mission variants kept
everyone too busy to contemplate the odds.

The primary force could level a small city in short order,
but it might not be enough. Their leader was the strongest

earthmover available: a reservist whose control was precise enough to make rock flow like water. She was backed up by three Tees from Lone Star company and two pyros from NYC. Their potential opponent was magnitudes more powerful than all of them put together.

Please let the threat window pass, Kris prayed once more, after finishing a scenario that left her and Sergeant Coby a hundred yards from the rest of the team. *Let it be a false alarm.*

She jumped six inches when the sergeant said, "You ready for this, Stan?"

"I'm here, aren't I?" Her temper spiked. She'd been transferred to a shitbird squad and stuck with a collar after *that night*, while Coby had gotten a promotion out of the incident. And now he was questioning her readiness. There was only so much unfairness a woman could swallow.

She snapped, "Why are you always riding my ass? You've been on my back ever since Day One when you went and told the whole squad to call me *Stan*. Why did you have to go and embarrass me like that? Do you know what it did to me?"

A few of the other newbies had used that name against her at every opportunity. They'd embraced the slur against her femininity, wearing down her belief in herself. Encouraged by her silence, the predators nipped and chivvied her until she was exhausted—and then they'd pulled her down.

Not her fault, her counselor kept telling her, but she still wondered what would've happened if she'd stood up for herself from the start. And now she wondered, *why is he letting me get away with this now?*

Coby looked down. "I didn't see it, no. Not until too late. I never meant—it was the teeth, that's all."

"Teeth? What about them?" Instantly she saw his slashing fangs, splashing blood everywhere, heard his bass voice roaring, bestial with fury, saw bright eyes maddened with pain and humiliation, locking with hers across a white tile floor smeared with red. Felt the burning power of his rampage carry her into a wild place where only violence and destruction existed.

She bit her tongue, fighting the flashback. Comprehension burst through her on the metallic taste of blood. K had been the toughest consonant to relearn after rollover. Some Tees never mastered the way it slid the tongue along the side fangs.. *Good Lord. He was trying to choose nicknames that were easier to say.*

"You're hesitating," Coby said abruptly. "Tonight. That's why I'm asking. You freeze up any time I'm near you. If I remind you too much—if you can't focus— I'll stand you down."

The threat shocked her. If he excluded her and the others died, how would she live with herself?

Wait. It isn't a threat. It's an offer. If Coby sidelined her, then she would be safe, as safe as possible, anyway. He was trying to go easy on her.

For the first time, she wondered if Coby felt the same guilt everyone kept telling her that she shouldn't feel. She looked down at the top of his helmet, at the vulnerable back of his lightly-armored neck, and she knew the answer. She hadn't been the only victim that night.

Her tears ran down her throat because her eyes no longer allowed them to spill out. "I don't hate you for not saving me," she said. "It wasn't your fault. I should've stopped them before it got out of hand."

When the sergeant looked up, his expression was full of shocked anger. "That's bullshit. I should've seen you were at risk. I should've put those fuckers on report the first time one of them made a pass. I should've kicked —"

Kris raised a hand, and he stopped speaking. *God, he really is young. He tried so hard, just like I did.*

Her attackers had been sentenced and executed. Maybe it was time to bury all the should-haves with them. Her heart thudded hard, and muscles shifted under her skin. "I'm in, Sarge. I won't freeze, I swear. Count on me."

Coby's face slowly went blank as he watched her, until his expression hardened to the steady, impersonal mask Kris was used to seeing. Then he nodded. "Okay. Good."

The ground underfoot quivered, the air rumbled, and the earth shook hard. Above the horizon to the south, the sky glowed red, under-lighting a plume of gray smoke. Lightning splayed through the smoke. The lieutenant's voice spoke in Kris's helmet speaker, crackling with static. "Team One, you're a go."

Less than ten minutes later, he said, "Team Two, move to Point Charlie. Containment and 'port-out both failed. We have a standoff. Engage on judgment."

Point Charlie was a slight rise outside the Fort Atkinson camp gates. Their access porter missed the altitude and brought them in twenty feet too high. Kris sank to her ankles in frozen dirt on landing. Coby and Amy crashed down on her left.

Snow lifted around them in a whirlwind as their air elemental—Private Erica Rasmussen, from North Dakota by way of Empire Company— brought herself and their three extraction porters safely to earth. Then she collapsed into a snow bank with a cry of pain.

The exit porters started cursing their absent compatriot

over the radio. Kris lifted the air elemental clear of her snowy nest. "Ankle?"

"No. Backlash. I'm drained. Oh, shizzle." The woman bent double and clutched her head with both hands. "Ouch. Pug knuckles, that hurts."

"Fast thinking." Coby halted beside Kris. Steam rose off his armor where snow had melted already. "I was sure we'd be cleaning up porter pancakes."

Kris realized with a stab of jealousy that the sergeant had recovered from a worse landing than hers, checked on the teleporters, and oriented himself in the time it took her to help the Private Rasmussen stand up.

Practice makes perfect, she reminded herself, and thought of how many times she'd said that after her daughter's skating lessons, after cheering for her son at track meets, after clapping at debate competitions. Coby had been a Marine most of his life. He'd had a lot of practice landing on his feet.

Rasmussen said, "I'm empty, Sarge. I'm a close-in specialist, not a force generator."

"You saved lives. All that matters. Hold here with the go teams." He looked down the hill. "You never would've had a chance for a chokeout anyway. Look at that."

Kris followed his gaze. Just outside the camp gates, a standard visitation bus had run off the road and sunk to the wheel wells in mud. That stretch of road—a hundred feet in front and a hundred behind the bus—now sat at the bottom of a crater with sheer, raw walls at least thirty feet high.

A bright fountain of lava bubbled up from the ground a few yards in front of the vehicle. The surface of the fluid was cooling to black, but it still crackled orange within, and it was piling up in mounds that crept in worm-like lines towards the bus.

Steam and smoke rose in clouds from the disrupted earth and the lava flow, obscuring most details, but the bus's gray and white paint scheme made it stand out. The roof had a charred hole in it, right in the center. A woman dressed in nothing but a glowing cloud of power stood beside that opening, gesturing up at the trio of Tees and the earthmover at the top of the cliff.

"That," Sergeant Coby said, "is one hell of a standoff. Where are the pyros?"

Amy joined them and pointed to two lumps in the roiled earth near the bus. The air above them shimmered, hot enough to dispel the rising fog. "There, I'll bet. She got the jump on them."

"That's...bad," Coby said. "We'd best plan on hunkering down for the K-strike. Be nice if we could bring out those passengers first, though."

Down below, the conversation between the primary team and Grace Bell was inaudible, but the screams and cries of the bus's remaining occupants carried up the hill on a hot, stinking breeze. Even as Kris took in the scene, those voices got weaker and fell silent. Her stomach knotted up. Her daughter had done a whole science fair project on volcanoes once. She'd been fascinated by all the various ways an eruption could kill people.

She whirled back to Rasmussen. "Do you have anything left, Private? There's gas coming up with that lava. They're dying, down there."

Rasmussen groaned and got to her feet, only to flop down with a wince a second later. "I fed in a little oh-two, pulled some gasses out. Gave 'em a few minutes maybe."

Sergeant Coby keyed his field radio. "We need air reserve

in the hot zone, LT. Any and all air that can be spared. One with wings would be nice."

"Negative," came the response. "They're needed for camp evac. Zeus is ready to roll, and the satellite clears horizon in five mikes. Move in to keep the target distracted, keep your exit lines clear."

Sergeant Coby pressed the radio to his forehead. Kris stifled a mixed impulse to either to pat him on the shoulder or burst into tears. A moment later, Coby said, "Goodie, Stan, on me. Let's go pretend to be backup."

INCIDENT SITE, NEAR FORT ATKINSON, KANSAS

A quick jog brought them to the edge of the crater just as two small figures emerged from the bus to sit at Grace's feet. The fog was rising to the bus roof now. Kris could barely see the children, but she could imagine them all too clearly.

She knew the faces that went with wails like the ones she was hearing. Their eyes would be squeezed tight shut against the unfairness of the world, mouths full of white baby teeth opened wide to cry out all the misery ever felt, and their faces would be streaked with dirt and tears.

Down in that fog, Grace Bell shouted, "Please, oh, please, someone help us! I don't want this. I didn't mean to do any of this. Please don't let me hurt anyone else. Can't someone stop this? Please save my babies. I only wanted to go home. I only want to go home and stop feeling this. Please make it *stop*."

Kris's heart broke, listening to that plea, and when she looked away, she saw the earthmover from Team One crying without shame. The woman had dramatic gray eyes in a dark brown face, and her features were crumpled with a grief that looked as deep as the emotion ripping through Kris's chest.

The earthmover's lips were moving. "Poor babies," she was saying, over and over. "Poor, poor babies."

"Help me," Grace Bell screamed, and the world shuddered beneath their feet and kept on shaking.

An idea hit Kris out of nowhere. She pushed aside doubts about the cost. It would save lives even if it failed in part, so the attempt had to be made.

Everyone who became collateral damage in a kinetic strike would leave behind lives and families. People were trapped here. In the bus. In the camp. Too many would never be evacuated in time. She could save them. It was that simple.

"We can stop this," she said to the earthmover, glancing at her badge. "Corporal Evans. You and me. You're a stonecaller, right? You're blocking as much as you can, but she's too strong, right? You're too far away. What if I get you closer? Will you help me save those babies?"

Evans nodded fast. "How?"

"We go in. You shield us, I get her up where it's cold and airless and there's no earth to keep pushing at her. She's out of control now. Maybe she gets herself together. Maybe not. At least she gets a chance, and if it doesn't work—well."

If the worst happened, only Kris and Grace would come burning down through the atmosphere, not the rock the Zeus satellite was maneuvering into place now. The fringe benefit was that they could be aimed somewhere safe and perhaps, if they were both lucky, be recovered and isolated.

But no matter what, it would have to happen somewhere else, which meant getting right down into the action. "You up for this, Corporal Evans?"

"Yes." Evans took a deep breath. "Let's do it. Gotta be fast."

"Sarge," Kris said, turning to Coby. "I have an idea."

He was listening to something, head down, nodding. He

held up a finger: *wait one.* Amy looked down at Kris with narrowed eyes. She stood head and shoulders over the sergeant, looming at his back like a guardian statue. *Wait,* she mouthed.

A chunk of the crater's raw earth wall broke and slid loose like a calving glacier.

Kris's lips lifted off her teeth in an involuntary snarl. The time to wait was over. She hit the radio channel for the exit porters back on the hilltop. "Exit, Corporal Stanislav. I need a quick-and-dirty lift to that bus, and five seconds after, I'll need a boost straight up. How high can you send me?"

"For fuck's sake, don't you people talk to each other? Ben just told your sergeant we can put one of you in orbit if you want," came the dry response. "Problem is that we can't guarantee you'll hit the bus, and we sure can't bring you back. No line of sight, no radio beacon, no—"

"No time to argue. On my mark, send me and my passenger in. Five seconds, take me and a passenger out to the edge of atmosphere."

Kris pulled Evans into a tight embrace with one arm. The ground underfoot shook harder, and a low rumble built in the air. "Get satellite tracking on us ASAP, after. I don't think we'd survive reentry."

"Uh—say again, private? Send *you* in, with Evans there?"

Kris snapped, "Yes, us. Do your damned job. On my mark."

"Shit," the porter said. "Okay, your funeral."

Amy had stopped eavesdropping on Coby's conversation and started listening to Kris. She was shaking her head.

No time to waste. Kris lifted her free hand in farewell. "Mark."

The world slid sideways, and she was standing in fog that reeked like rotten eggs in a hot locker room. There was nothing in front of her. She spun around. Evans yelped as she was swung off her feet, and then Kris was staring at the bright glowing form of Grace Bell. The woman was being swallowed alive by power she could not contain.

"Help," she whispered, and her children screamed.

Evans hummed a note under her breath. The bus listed sideways, and the children shrieked again, carried away from their mother on a rising mass of pale, crackling stone. Kris leaped for Grace, and the wall of cool rock kept rising behind the other woman like a breaking wave.

Stone came crashing down around them both just as the world slid sideways again. Rock pressed into Kris from all sides like a giant's hand, squeezing tight. She hadn't noticed the porter cursing in her radio earpiece until his voice abruptly cut off.

The stony cocoon loosened to a shell at arm's length as Grace's power flared. Kris took a breath, amazed that she could breathe. Air from rock: only one or two R-series rollovers in history had ever come into that kind of power.

Her stomach and her ears sloshed, and dizziness washed over her. Gravity was barely a force, gently pulling her backwards as if she was halfway falling into nowhere. This time, the targeting on the teleport must've been perfect.

Grace flailed, kicking and screaming, and it took every bit of Kris's self-control to keep from crushing her in self-defense. The woman was tiny and as soft as a pillow. Kris could have beaten her in a fight even before she hit rollover and changed into what she was now.

She let her own power rise, edging to the precipice of full rampage. Then she made her arms and body into a cage, containing Grace the way she'd held Matty when he was a toddler throwing tantrums.

"Shh," she said. "I've got you. Calm down. Don't stretch that stone too thin, there's nothing outside but space. Be calm. Ride the power, they tell us Tees. Can't be too different for you. Get a grip on it, and everything will be fine."

"Oh—oh—oh!" Grace shivered as if she was freezing to death, but her body was feverish hot. "I couldn't bear it, I had to get out, and oh, God, he said no, I had to stay, and they made me get off the bus, and I got so angry, and—I killed him, and the world started coming apart, and I can't. I can't. I killed him, didn't I? What am I going to do?"

"Be strong," Kris said. "I don't know who you killed, but your kids are alive, and they need their mother. Don't leave them alone."

"I can't," Grace whispered. The shivers got worse, and the soft flesh against Kris's arms began to harden. "It's too late for me. I can feel it coming up inside. It's going to come out. There's too much of it and not enough of me."

"Just hold on. It won't last forever. You can be as strong as you need to be," Kris said, but strength didn't guarantee survival, nor did willpower. Nothing did. Power was notoriously fickle, manifesting in unpredictable ways, and sometimes it drowned those it rolled over.

Grace whimpered, and her body shook until the tremors became one long unending spasm. She kept getting hotter too, until everywhere their bodies touched felt as if it was about to burst into flames. Kris growled and let herself tip into full rampage as smoke rose off her armor.

Her vision sharpened and went red around the edges, and the pain disappeared. Her body sang with strength, and she felt invulnerable.

Grace turned, pulling in her legs, and rested a hand against Kris's shoulder. The armor sizzled and popped.

"Thank you," she whispered. "Thank you for saving them. Thank you for being here with me at the end. Tell them I'm sorry I couldn't stay. I am sorry."

And then she melted away, flaring bright orange and then white-hot, molten and excruciating. The flow splashed over Kris's throat and mouth, smothering her screams, and then the stone shell around her shattered, bursting outward in a powdery, soundless explosion. Before she lost consciousness, she saw stars in their millions, spangled across a velvet black sky.

AFTERMATH, NEAR FORT ATKINSON, KANSAS

Dawn cast a warm pink glow over white snow and torn black soil before the recovery team brought a scorched lump of fused rock and flesh safely back to earth. The mass came to rest near the center of a huge clearing which had been a crater a few hours earlier. Murmurs rose from a waiting crowd. A scattering of hesitant applause followed.

Jack Coby shouldered his way to the front of the officers and journalists who had gathered on short notice for this event. They wouldn't have given way for him, a lowly sergeant, but in front of him walked Colonel Galloway and Lieutenant Akron. Today, for once, everyone was giving Mercury Battalion's commander and her chosen representatives the respect they deserved.

The previous night had been the worst outbreak of uncontrolled power incidents since the first wave of rollovers in the forties. Tens of thousands had died on that long-ago day, and the property damage climbed into the millions of dollars before the accounting was done.

Last night's casualty count was under twenty, nationwide,

and even the land here at ground zero of the worst containment was on its way back to normal only hours later. Mercury Battalion had done itself proud, and it was only right that its commander be first on the scene for the return of one of her own.

Kris's sacrifice had saved thousands at the very least. That fact might be enough, Jack thought, to someday forgive her for doing it. Right now, only exhaustion was keeping him off an emotional cliff. If one more person congratulated him on his quick thinking and command ability, he was going to hurt someone.

Behind him came the rest of the Gateway Company personnel who'd been scrambled for the containment here. They were somber, as befitted the occasion, but their heads were up, their faces shining with pride, and in most cases with tears. They were here to bring home their fallen.

Retrieving a human-sized object from high-atmosphere before it burned up on re-entry had taken the coordinated efforts of two teleporters, three telekinetics and two flight-capable air elementals. The mixed National Guard and civilian DPS team stood in a huddle around the object of their efforts.

As the last elemental landed, he spread his wings wide, hiding the scene from all the prying, curious eyes. A moment later, the retrieval team leader turned and yelled out, "MEDIC!"

MARINE CAMP BUTLER, ELGIN, ILLINOIS

Kris hadn't expected to wake up, but she did.

Every part of her body hurt. Her teeth hurt. Her feet hurt. Even her eyebrows hurt. There were enough aches in enough places to make her tremble with panicky memories, and that brought her trembling to the edge of rampage, with power pulsing into her veins.

Power smothered the worst of the pain, and some of the scabbed burns that covered her from her stinging scalp to her sore toes began to tingle and heal. She took her time sitting up and setting aside flashes of the past.

Once she was vertical, she swallowed a fresh wave of emotional pain that had nothing to do with her current troubles. Then she gently put all the guilt and the grief back in their boxes.

She went to tuck a curl of hair behind her ears but found only bare skin and more scabs. Her head was bare, and her eyebrows hurt because they were gone.

As soon as she looked around the room, she recognized it as one of the Tee-series isolation rooms in the sick bay back at Camp Butler. Unless all Tee-series hospital rooms were built from the same blueprint, which she supposed was possible. Anything was possible. She wasn't dead. She marveled at that miracle, and then she wondered, *how long have I been asleep?*

Had she missed her weekly video call with Eryka and Matty? Had someone told her children about the mission? Who had broken the news to Grace Bell's family? Had the poor woman left behind a husband? Parents? Siblings? Who was taking care of her children?

Kris got all the questions lined up just as a familiar corpsman came into the room carrying two steaming bowls of porridge on a tray. Each of the bowls was as big as the woman's head. Kris thought the corpsman's name was Farina, but she peeked at the badge just to be sure.

Nothing was making much sense any more.

"Hey, Private," Corpsman Farina said. "Let's stop meeting like this, okay?"

"Okay. Am I dead?" Kris asked. "Because I feel very odd."

"It's a normal kind of odd. Last time, your head got squished too, so this part was over before you woke up." The corpsman smiled and checked on assorted lines of fluid and dials, marking everything in her little book. "Your body heals fastest in rampage, so you'll keep cycling as often as your cells can manage it. It'll be a while. They had to trigger you twice on-scene to get your lungs healed enough to breathe properly. Rest, ride the surges, and eat up."

She handed over the bowls. The nutrient paste tasted horrible, but Kris felt better when it was inside her instead of the bowls. After the meal she was left alone in the room again, alone in her big, white, soft bed with nothing but fluffy white pillows and her thoughts for company.

It was not a fun party.

Someone knocked at the door, jolting her awake from a nightmare of flame and smoke. She blinked away tears, smoothed a hand over her scalp, and touched a half-inch of soft new hair. She touched her face next, and was pleased with the result. She was a monster, but she had eyebrows.

Sergeant Coby stopped at the foot of the bed and frowned at her. He was feeling moody judging by his hardened skin, and his voice was hard too. "Good job. That's what I'm s'posed to say, but what I want to say, is, what the fuck were you thinking? I had it under control until you jumped in."

Kris let Coby's anger roll right off her because none of the words made much sense. "I get that you're mad I acted without orders," she said, "but for the rest of it, you're going to have to use real small words. I'm dead stupid today."

"You were nearly dead-dead." Coby's shoulders drooped,

and he looked around the room. There were no Tee-safe chairs, so he put his back to the wall and put his hands in his pockets. "This stays off the record, Stan. Got it? Just you and me and the truth."

She nodded. Confusion bubbled higher, followed by fear, and she rode out a swooping tingle of rampage that channeled itself into healing.

Coby said quietly, "I was gonna do what you did—take her up and out to save the rest—but the exit team leader kept asking me questions, and you snuck in behind my back. You were smarter, too. I never would've scooped up Evans. That was brilliant."

Kris shook her head. The odd conversation with the exit 'porters made more sense when she added Sergeant Coby's confession to the timeline, but the rest was still baffling. "You would've gone up without cover? Why would you do that?"

Teleported into near-vacuum without any protection, Grace would have been dead in moments, but Coby would have died too. Not even a T1 like Amy could survive for more than a few minutes in space. Coby was only a T5 and on the fragile side of that, due to the Y variation.

Kris had taken a calculated risk. Coby would've been committing suicide.

The sergeant slouched and glared. Kris dared to glare back. She hadn't asked him to come here and be confusing.

He cleared his throat before speaking. "I turn twenty-three next week."

Now she was totally lost. "So what?"

"The world record for early onset longevity is age twenty-three years, four months, two days."

"Oh." Kris didn't know what else to say. She'd forgotten about the dark side of Coby being so young and already past rollover. It was one of those things no one talked about, and that made it easier to forget.

She'd never thought about what a burden that knowledge must be to bear in silence. She wouldn't forget again.

Coby laughed. "Yeah, *oh*. I'm a dead man walking. I have been for months now. I figured, of all of us there I had the least to lose, and so I thought, *well, fuck it. Why not?* But then you went. You. You have kids, Stan. Did you think of them?"

He sounded angry again, but it wasn't frightening angry. It was the kind of angry that made Kris want to pat him on the head and tell him how sweet he was, which would probably get her killed or court-martialed.

She pursed her lips. "What I thought was that everybody there had family, Sergeant Jackass. Even you."

Coby bent his knees and slid to the floor, looking defeated. "Everyone kept patting me on the back, congratulating me on my balls for ordering you up like that—and I couldn't explain that you'd been an insubordinate bitch, not when it saved so many people. When the air crew found your pulse—"

He stopped and swallowed again. "When you stabilized and kicked into independent healing, all I could think was, Thank God, LT won't have to write notification letters. Thank God I won't have to help deliver them and tell lies to your children. I still haven't written up a report. Cap's ready to ream me a new one."

"I'm glad I'm awake to talk sense to you, then," Kris said. "Take the credit. You deserve it. You trained me. A commendation won't get me through my hitch and home to my family any faster. If you want to haggle about it, then take me back into your squad when you get my request. That's the price of my silence."

The sound Coby made teetered on the balance point between a sigh and a laugh. "Okay, then," he said, and shoved himself upright again. The wall crunched behind him. "Okay. We're good?"

"We're good." Kris said. A yawn came up from nowhere, and three more followed before she got the reflex under control.

Coby waved off her attempted apology. "You're in sick bay. Get back to resting and healing. I'll have Goodie bring by some transfer paperwork tomorrow."

Kris nestled deeper into the big white pillows and yawned again. "Excellent," she said. "When she gets here we can start planning your birthday party."

ROUNDUP

THE PROUD ONES DIED FIRST. They died in the exam rooms, they died on the train platform behind the intake offices, and they died standing in the hot sun as they waited for a ride to oblivion. They refused to disrobe, defied the orders of their uniformed kidnappers, and demanded water and shade. Pride was a sin, and they paid for their transgressions with their lives.

Ruth remembered her Scripture in time to save her life. *Patience is better than pride*, the Bible taught. When the government thugs came for her with their legal papers, their uniforms, and their red, sweaty faces, she bowed her head and opened the door. While the thugs drank sweet iced tea and mocked her daughter's crooked shelves and small treasures, Ruth packed the one bag the law allowed her to bring, and then she hugged her grandchildren and kissed her daughter's salt-wet cheek.

She would not be provoked in spirit even when the thugs grew bored with the farewells. They pulled her from her family and called her *old nigger bitch* in front of her grandchildren, but she lowered her eyes and swallowed pride. Humility was a frail shield, but it was all she had. She consoled herself with the hidden truth. She might be an old bitch, but that made her a cunning old dog who could learn new tricks. Her time would come. There was a time for everything, under the sun.

The thugs brought her to the government building, where she was inspected by men who looked at computer screens more than her naked form. She was humble, they were indifferent, and they passed her back to the thugs with stamps and papers that were promptly taken away, as her bag had been.

The rules of this new existence seemed simple enough, and not much different than the ones that had governed her old life. Never expect help, never challenge authority, never show weakness, never rebel. Disrespect was death. Weakness was death. The silent and the strong survived.

She wanted to survive. She had been patient all her life, and her time would come soon. The official diagnosis only gave numbers and labels to what anyone with eyes could see; even as Ruth's womb had shriveled and her hair turned gray, God had touched her body with strange new blessings.

Old nigger bitch, the thugs called her, but her skin was whiter than theirs now. She was changing, and that was what they feared most. Weeks past, her wrinkled skin had begun to peel like the bark of a sycamore tree, leaving pale tender flesh exposed. Silence would be easy now. The shifts within her body had stolen the voice she once raised in joy with the church choir every Sunday.

She would have other powers to replace the lost skill, if she completed this metamorphosis that came to the old and killed the proud. Rollover, the thugs and bureaucrats called it, like a command to a pet, or a sleepy stretch in bed, but it fell where it pleased, and it was not restful. No one understood why or how it happened, but everyone knew one thing: some of those God touched were given talents beyond human understanding.

This mystery was dividing the world the same way every other transformation in history had split it: into the wanted and the unwanted; the haves and the have-nots; the privileged and the oppressed. Ruth would be sequestered while she changed because that was the law for those who could make no other arrangements. The poor and unwanted were exiled to places where the system could do its best to destroy them, out of sight, out of mind.

Power in the hands of the powerless threatened the status quo, and authority fought against disruption. Legislators had passed laws to keep the downtrodden from profiting from new abilities, police enforced laws that pulled lives and families apart, and judges gave the scraps to their friends and followers. It wasn't the way the laws were supposed to work, but they twisted in the hands of the unscrupulous and the greedy. Life was not fair. Evil was real.

Ruth had been praying for deliverance from evil all her life. That would change, if she lived, and so she prayed for time and patience. She would deliver herself, if she survived this test.

She wasn't the weirdest of the lost souls reaped together by government hands on that day. The doctors and the bookkeepers called the group a cohort, as if they were ancient Roman soldiers going off to war, not prisoners torn unwilling from homes and family. Ruth's crop started off fifty strong, at the intake office. By the time the train arrived, after the long hours spent standing in a line, bags at their feet—silent, hungry, thirsty—their count stood at forty-four.

If they had been Roman soldiers, decimated for punishment, they would have lost fewer.

One man arrived with stubby wings springing bloody from his shoulders, raw and half-formed. He raised his voice at a doctor, and the thugs broke him into pieces in front of the rest. One woman could not walk without the ground turning hot and fluid beneath her feet. If she had been patient, she might have raised a volcano from the sea in time, but she begged, please help, when she slipped and slid on the train platform.

The guards shot her in the face and flamed her body to ash there in the sunshine.

Two more of the prideful complained of the heat and were shot where they stood. One woman simply evaporated, to the consternation of her neighbors. She might have called hurricanes to her hands, if she had held herself together a little longer, but she looked around with despair in her eyes and turned her power on herself.

Ruth could feel power moving in her bones like seeds moving under dark soil. She would wait. Her time would come. When the door to the boxcar shut behind the last of the intake cohort, she made her way to the corner by the water barrel, and then she sat down and prayed.

The weak ones died next. The air in the train car was thick and rank, and the noise of the rails came through a splintered wood floor that shook underfoot. Vicious flies bit and stung every bit of skin they could find reach, and the doors never opened, when the train stopped once, and then again. They shared the water, equal lots to all, dignified and civilized to the end, but the water did not last. The cold night seeped in, the motion rattled their teeth in their heads, and when the sun rose again, the metal walls grew hot enough to blister skin.

The head count of the living, when the doors finally opened to daylight again, fell to thirty-eight.

More died on the long hike from the train through sharp grasses and dunes to the seashore. Their guards rode on little cars with wide tires and engines that buzzed like the flies, and those who fell behind, stayed behind, ashes smoking in the sand. At the end of the trail they came to a pier that jutted far into the water, well beyond the lapping waves.

The long tongue of fiberglass and metal aimed its impudent length at the black line of an island on the horizon, and two more thugs scuffed back and forth along its sandy surface. These two were matched like Adam and Eve, man and woman dressed alike in gray short sleeves and darker trousers.

Swim for it, the thugs said, and laughed when most of their victims sat down on the beach and waited to die. Ruth dropped her bag and walked to the water's edge. The odors of rotted fish and living ocean rose to her nostrils, and the gentle surf filled her ears with a murmuring song of yielding strength and swelling power.

"Don't be damned fools," said one of the guards from the pier, but he was not speaking to Ruth. He said to the thug escorts, "Haven't you done enough damage already? Nobody needs the hassle of an investigation on top of the loss reports."

"Sit and rest," he said to the cohort. "The boat is coming. Sit and wait. Don't worry. The worst is almost over. Everything will be better once you get to the camp. Hold on. We've radioed for transport."

Was it sympathy in his voice? Pity? Ruth wanted no part of the man's emotion, whatever it was. She wanted no part of this thug or his precious system, that might work for people like him but took everything from people like her. She wanted power and freedom, so she smiled and nodded, and she bided her time in silence.

No one died while they waited to be carried over the water to exile. They were given water and food from locked boxes, and they were told to sit, and rest, and walk as they wished. Interns, the pier guards called them, assigning them the status of innocent youngsters apprenticed to a trade, and the travel escort thugs were ordered to set up canopies for shade.

Plastic sheets and supports came from a shed nestled into the dunes and built a shelter. The thugs grumbled, and they kicked sand, but they followed their orders, and shade was offered.

Ruth chewed on bitter insight along with the food, and swallowed it down with cool water. This new man and woman, they were as dangerous in their own way as the others.

Kindness could be as effective a weapon as pain—more so, when relief was offered in opposition to abuse.

Comfort and flattery could tempt the strong into docile cooperation. Charity could be sweet bait around a poisonous core.

Ruth ate and drank and smothered gratitude in its cradle. She was neither an intern nor a soldier, and she would not be tempted into forgetting herself.

She was one of God's fools, culled from the aged and the infirm to demonstrate His glory to His people. She deserved more than shade and sandwiches, and she needed no one's pity. She would not be so easily seduced into befriending the enemy.

Two boats came over the sea to the pier. They were sleek and deadly, with dark metal cannons on front and back. Their high cabins bristled with antennae, and windows gleamed bright. A whole new cadre of guards stood along the deck rails. Dark faces as well as pale ones regarded the arriving prisoners with hard eyes and tight mouths.

Ruth's companions in exile were as varied in race as they were in their strangeness, but until now, their tormentors had been uniformly white as they were uniformly dressed in gray. That was the way of the world. This new development disturbed her like nothing else she had yet seen.

That the oppressed had embraced hatred was a bitter truth to swallow. She carried it like a sharp stone in her stomach, and she prayed she might someday find the strength to forgive them.

The boat crew loaded the cohort aboard and sat them on the deck in the blazing sun. Only crew allowed below, the new guards said, and the apologies in their voices rang out like a discordant chiming of bells.

There were rules here too, and the guards' devotion to those rules left no room for humanity.

No matter their sex, their race, their pasts, they were thugs first, humans last. Ruth ignored their guilty frowns and watched the pier guards and the original escort recede across foam-flecked waves.

Sea spray tickled her face, and the hum of the engine lulled her into a doze as one shore fell behind and the other grew in front. Her belly was full, and the sun was warm but no longer a searing force.

Power pumped through her veins and moved inside her flesh much the same way that her infant daughters had kicked

long ago. A sense of serenity fell over her, and she drifted on
the waves of life and growth.

She came back to herself when someone jostled her elbow.
The woman to her right tipped herself back, over the rails and
into the sea. She smiled as she went down, and she sank fast,
but not fast enough.

The thugs manning the back of the boat stood and
shouted, the front settled with a hiss of foam as the driver
slowed, and the guns coughed.

The ocean plumed up in huge gouts and fell in a curtain of
cool spray. Fish rose in the boat's wake, bellies and bodies
distorted, like miniature replicas of the dead woman's
rounded form. The thugs brought her into the boat with gaffs,
hooking her flesh with the sharp, merciless points, and they
carried her body below decks in silence. The engines roared
again, and the boat moved on.

If only the woman had been patient a little longer, Ruth
thought again, and she let herself mourn, because there was a
time for that, too.

Soon, there would be a time to learn the names of the dead
and hear them sung to the heavens. The time would come
when she would reap what had been sowed in her heart
this day.

THREE MONTHS into a life bounded by bells and blared
shouts, painted lines and painful lessons in failure to
conform, Ruth stood at her bunk and prepared for inspection.
Her bare wet skin ached from the ragged scrub brush, and the
high-pressure shower had left new bruises across her shoulder. Her scalp itched, and her hair, brittle from harsh soaps,
split and crumbled away.

She was as bald as a stone now, all but one thin patch of fuzz at the base of her neck that refused to surrender. She smoothed clean sheets onto the thin mattress that smelled of disinfectant, sweat and pain, folded her clean clothes atop the sheets, and knelt naked beside the bed.

This was her favorite time of day, this quiet pause between the back-to-bunks bell and call for the morning's first head count. Silence ruled the dorm by mutual agreement during this short respite. Ruth used the precious moments to say her silent prayers and nurture a little peace within her soul.

The road to hell was paved with bunk inspections, physical examinations, and countless other daily indignities. The island internment camp was staffed by people so committed to their cause that they were blind to their sins. The degradation they inflicted was impersonal, born from dedication to routine rather than malice. The humiliations were a matter of regulation, not evil intent.

The guards did not mean to be cruel. They did not even mean to be guards. They called themselves counselors.

They were hateful in a million ways they never saw because they meant well. They were rude and brusque, not vindictive, but they valued efficiency above all else and efficiency was a cruel taskmaster.

Ruth remembered little of the intake processing. The orders and questions had blurred past without time for understanding. She moved from station to station with the rest of her battered fellows, gathering equipment and lessons in procedure without comprehending any of it. Hours disappeared in a blur of announcements and questions, ending in assignment to this duty or that, based on past employment and ability to work.

The counselors insisted that the purpose of the camp was

to induct the newly-changed into the mysteries of their new abilities. They believed in themselves and their mission, even as their every action undermined and belied their encouraging words.

Interns were expected to master their new talents without being taught how those talents worked. They were set up for failure, and when they failed, they were blamed for their laziness and their lack of ambition.

Exploration learning, the guards called it, and refused to interfere unless—until—their charges' lives were in danger

Even with those obstacles to overcome, the cohort learned from and with each other. Slowly, ever so slowly, Ruth learned to tap into the warm power she could feel still growing, still maturing, within her.

It told her its name in the dark, hot nights after curfew. She made its acquaintance through the voices of frogs and the whine of mosquito wings. God was filling her with the fullness of the world.

Songs of stone and wood, air and water would be hers to sing. Souls would be hers to move. Miracles would answer to her heart's call—if she lived.

She kept her growing knowledge to herself and bent her neck to the yoke. Any rebellion, however small, generated an immediate, uncompromising response. First offenses resulted in punishment– physical, painful and public. Any further infractions–any infraction–resulted in counseling. No one who returned from that office committed a third infraction. They came back to their bunks with slack faces and empty eyes, and they were models of proper behavior forever after.

Ruth bent her head, and prayed as she did every morning, for the patience to endure one more day, for her transformation to reach its end, and for deliverance from counseling.

The sympathetic, smiling men and women who stripped the souls from their victims were the only enemies on the island that she truly feared.

She made no friends. Alliances were dangerous.

After watching lovers join and pairs bond only to be counseled into docile propriety, she resigned herself to wandering alone in this wilderness. And since she was alone she recited the names of the fallen to herself, to keep them vivid in her memory. There would be a time for them.

Inspection went well that morning. No one was beaten. Only one woman was taken away for punishment. The insults and accusations were bitter to swallow, but swallow them Ruth did. She dressed and followed her bunkmates to breakfast, where they ate not nearly enough, and there she received her duty for the day: beachcombing.

The chore of cleaning storm debris from the shoreline was a torture and a reward as closely bound together as a chunk of tender meat marbled with gristle. Her power grew steadier whenever she walked barefoot on the earth, near the whispering dune grasses, but the labor tore her flesh and racked her aging joints.

The ranks of her crew were composed of others equally challenged, and they were set the task of moving an uprooted tree at the high edge of the tideline. Find your gifts, they were told. Reach deep. Push yourselves. Don't be lazy.

There were others in the camp who could already move heavy objects with the force of their will. They had been given other tasks, requiring skills that would not come easily to them. The counselors were not interested in teaching mastery or providing practice, no matter what they said. They cultivated suffering.

So Ruth and the rest rolled the log by hand, back to the sea through the stubborn sands. As they reached the wash of the surf, she felt something tear loose, deep inside. Her knees gave out as muscles spasmed in her belly, in her back.

She fell, crying in her soundless voice, and her palms scraped against the tree's splintered, soggy bark when it moved onward and she did not.

"She'll get up or she won't," one counselor said to another, while they watched her tremble helpless beneath the weight of the air. "You know the statute. No interference with the natural order. Call it in."

They left her there, lost between land and water, between the agony of consciousness and the solace of oblivion. No one spoke up, no good Samaritan came passing by.

Ruth lay on the sand, alone and abandoned, but in that dead silence, God smiled on her at last. Her power burst forth in fullness and glory. She pressed her hands against the wet earth full of a million crawling microscopic things and took the gift of creation and destruction into herself.

Her skin rippled and darkened as life tingled through her body. Aches and pains vanished as if they had never existed, and strength flowed into her limbs. She sat up, admiring beautiful walnut skin she had thought forever bleached.

Another thought, another wish, and she touched springy hair as soft as cotton, and she knew it would be as black as it had ever been in her long-ago youth. Next she chastised herself for the sins of selfishness and vanity, and she stood.

It was time. She gathered up the all the slights and the hurts, all the fears and humiliations, and anger rose in a whirlwind. She stood primed to release justice when a voice whispered in the silence at the eye of her storm.

She paused to listen.

Her daughter's new baby was laughing at sunbeams. Her grandson was singing.

The wind fell. Cold water lapped Ruth's toes. The sun burned down. She smiled.

The retribution of flood and fire was not hers to dispense. Vengeance belonged to the Lord.

She held death in her hands now, but she held life as well. She opened her mouth and raised her voice in thanks. Tears flowed down her face as she sang, drying in salt tracks on her skin before she was finished. She sang the oppressors back to shore, to their families, to contemplate their sins and find their own fates.

They had sown the wind, but the whirlwind would pass them over this once.

Ruth sang the souls back into the deadened hearts of the "counseled" next, and then she sang of cleansing, and healing, and life.

When she was done, the sky was twilight purple, and she was no longer alone.

Hands reached out to her, ears pricked up, and eyes in every shape and color stared at her amidst a crowd of bodies wondrous and commonplace. Shoulder to shoulder they stood, God's gifts on display, brought into their powers by hers.

They smiled and rejoiced with her, for they were free.

"What will we do?" someone asked.

"The Lord has brought us to this place," Ruth said. "We will make it ours."

LOCKDOWN

18 APRIL, 7:00 AM 1500 COTTONWOOD RD ELGIN, ILLINOIS

ELENA MORENO'S family wasn't normal. She wanted to be ordinary more than anything in the world, so every morning before school she checked her grocery lists and made breakfasts and lunches for her siblings. It was a lot of work, but id she didn't do it, no one would.

Her little sister already did as much as anyone could ask of an eight-year-old. Teresa could wake to an alarm and dress herself in the outfits they chose together before bedtime, and she could even get little Marco dressed and walk him to day care on her way to school.

She could do all that, but she wasn't old enough to trust alone with knives or the toaster. Elena still had to do the complicated, dangerous things so they could have all the things normal families did.

Papa was supposed to see the littles away to school, but he almost never stayed awake long enough in the mornings any

more. Someone had to do the necessary things, and since
Papa couldn't do them, Elena took care of what she could and
hoped nothing else went wrong.

On Friday morning, she sat alone in the kitchen and
scraped butter and the last of the jam onto a slice of toast.
Guilt turned every sweet bite to sour in her mouth. The jar
was supposed to last until Monday, but she'd used too much
all week, the way she always did. She wrote "strawberry
preserves" on the grocery list and hoped Papa didn't want
toast over the weekend. No one liked seeing him angry these
days.

The usual excuses ran through Elena's mind while she
packed up her lunch. It wasn't her fault she'd eaten too much.
She had track practice. Running burned calories. She was
thirteen. Her body was changing. She was growing. Nutrition
was important. It was only a little jam.

The excuses were all lies. The truth was simple: she
couldn't control her appetite. Tears stung her eyes as she
looked at her lunch bag: ten grapes in a bag; two chocolate-
chip cookies; two wraps, each with a swipe of beans, one
spoonful of salsa and a chicken slice. Too much.

Her breakfast made a hard lump of misery in her belly
until she put one cookie into Teresa's bag instead. She prayed
for strength every day, but sometimes she thought it might be
better if she'd never been born.

When headlights flashed through the gap between the
heavy curtains in the living room, she grabbed her books and
hurried towards the front door. The hall rug slipped under
her feet, throwing her off-balance, and her bag thumped
against the stair rail. The sound echoed through the quiet
house.

She froze, hoping it might be overlooked.

No such luck. Her father's voice rolled down the stairs. "Maria Elena Moreno, don't you dare leave this house without speaking to me."

His words were slurred, like always these days. Elena's heart began to pound as hard as if she was doing wind sprints. "Papa, Izzie's mom is here. I have to go."

"Mrs. Givens will wait. If she won't, I'll drive you to school myself. I told you last night that I wanted to see you before you left for school. Come up here right now."

Elena set down her bag and trudged upstairs. Her father's office door was cracked open, and the light from inside the room painted the hall carpet a rusty color like dried blood. She put a trembling hand on the door knob and went inside.

"I'm sorry, papa, I was trying to be quiet so I wouldn't disturb you." The words came out in a rush, and she kept her eyes down. The fear inside got bigger, and it pushed tears up into her eyes. "Please don't be angry."

The silence was agonizing. The sound of the chair moving under Papa's weight made Elena's knees go wobbly, and she wanted to throw up.

"Elena, I swear by all that's holy, I do not know what to do with you." Her father came closer, smelling of cinnamon and cologne. His shoes stopped right in front of her.

If I run away, what will he do? Will he chase me? She couldn't run. She was too scared to move.

"This can't go on, m'ija. You tiptoe around like a ghost, you eat less than a mouse, and every time I turn around, you're either locked in your room or running out the door. You are breaking my heart. Tell me what's wrong."

Elena's mouth went dry. "Nothing's wrong. You don't have to drive me. I can walk, if Izzie and her mom left already. It's fine."

Her father sighed. The force of it warmed Elena's scalp, where her braids left skin exposed. "You are ashamed of me, aren't you? Frightened and ashamed."

"No, Papa." Yes, she was scared and ashamed, and ashamed of being scared. She wanted a hug so badly that her whole body ached with the need, but her skin crawled at the idea of him touching her, and that fear was bigger. *Please don't touch me. Please don't.*

Her father retreated. The floorboards squeaked, and keys tapped. He said, "I've sent Mrs. Givens a message. She will wait. I don't know what to say. Maybe we should call your mama. It's already afternoon where she is. She wouldn't mind."

"No!" Elena said. *I don't want to bother her. I hate being a bother. I don't want to be noticed at all.* "She's busy. Don't make her upset. I don't want her worrying over me. I don't want to talk to anyone. Please, Papa. I have to go."

"Go where?" Papa came closer again. "I know it's testing week. The nurse called yesterday when she saw that your form wasn't signed. That is why you're so frightened, isn't it? It's brought all the memories back up. Tell me true, are you going to school or skipping school?"

Elena's heart sank. She had hoped Papa wouldn't find out until too late to stop her. "I can't do it, Papa. I don't want to know. I don't want to have to leave home like you and Mama did. I'm going to school, but I need to skip the test. I'm going to leave at lunch. Please don't be angry."

"I'm not angry." His voice turned hard. "I'm not, but it's the law. You can't run away from it. Think about Teresa and Marco. Do you want Public Safety to come here looking for you? Think of how much that would frighten them, after what happened to me. I need you to be responsible, m'ija.

Promise me you'll do your duty. It's only for screening, to see if you're at risk later. We all need to know. So. Give me your word, please."

Guilt washed though Elena again, and she felt too tired to keep arguing. She hadn't considered any of those things Papa had listed off. "I promise, Papa. I'll be good."

"Good." Papa sighed again. "I'm getting better, m'ija. I stay up later, every day. I've been awake to give Marco and Teresa hugs good-bye every day this week, and I walked Marco to school once. Today after I see them off, I'll go to the church and light a candle, and I'll pray that your mother and I didn't pass our curse to you."

Elena's heart swelled with all the emotions ever, and she looked up. "Oh, Papa. Thank you."

That's all she could get out before the lump in her throat got too large to talk around.

Her father's face made her want to run away and never look back. *Not my papa!* That was what her heart screamed.

Her papa had a broad brown face and a smile with small square teeth, and his shoulders were so wide that he could hold Elena in one arm and her sister in the other. This weird stranger had moon-glowing eyes, and his pale, narrow face gleamed in the dim light. His hair was a fine, white ruff that rose high over his pointy, twitchy ears.

He'd had a hand outstretched, hovering near Elena's cheek, but he dropped it to his side. His fingers were long and slim, not the thick strong hands that tossed Elena into the air when she was as young as Marco was. Claws at the fingertips flexed in their sheaths. When he spoke, the tips of his fangs showed.

"You take after me," he said in his lisping not-Papa voice. "When my date came up, last year, I told myself it wasn't important, that I didn't need to know. Your mother had only been home from quarantine a month, and I didn't want to leave you with only one parent again so soon. I appealed for delay after delay, and I told myself that this couldn't possibly happen to me. I was wrong."

His ears went back, drooping. Elena looked away. Her stomach went tight and queasy.

Papa said, "You were so brave, calling for help and hiding your sister and brother from me when I was crazy with the pain, but I—if I had done my duty, I would have spared you all of it. Your mother and I, we're both so proud of the way you handled it. You never should've seen what you did."

Elena shrugged, because she couldn't say, *I don't care if you're proud. I don't want to be brave. I don't want anyone to know I have freaks for parents. Resentment boiled up in her chest. I want my family back.*

At least Mama had still been Mama after her internment. She'd given everyone presents and hugs before she left, and when she came home she could fill the pool without a hose, and keep the rain off the roof, and make snow for sledding. She hadn't turned weird and weak and helpless.

Everything would be fine if Mama was home now, but she wasn't.

Papa went to his drafting desk, turned on his screen, and stared at his palettes and tools. He had a picture of Mama on the display, and he touched it with one finger. "I thank God that I was allowed early release when your Mama got drafted for the drought effort, but I wish—everything would be better, if she was here."

It hurt to hear her angry thoughts spoken aloud in that sad, soft voice. It made all her efforts seem pointless. *But I try so hard! Is it all for nothing?* Elena swallowed the pain. "Am I doing such a bad job? Aren't I taking care of things properly?"

"Oh sweetie. You are a blessing, but it isn't fair that you've had to grow up so fast. You do so much, and adjusting has been so much harder than I expected. Relying on you to make me lists and read bus schedules and guide me in the bright stores, taking care of Marco and Teresa when I can't ... it isn't right. The doctor says my vision will be day-safe soon. Things will get better. I want to go to the park with Teresa in the afternoons. I want to cheer you in your cross-country races next fall."

"You do?" *If you come and people see you, then everyone will know.* Elena bit her tongue and prayed that it wouldn't happen, and she knew she was the worst daughter ever, for having those thoughts. "You don't have to do that."

"Oh, Maria Elena." Her father closed his weird eyes and slumped in his seat. "I pray for so many things, but most of all I pray that you're a null and never see disgust and fear in your own child's eyes."

He sounded so sad, and it was easier to talk when he wasn't looking. Elena wrestled down her shame and found something to offer him. "We're out of strawberry jam. Maybe you could take me to do the shopping early this week? If we go tonight, and then to church after, we could pray together. I can ask Izzie to babysit if you want. I would like that."

Papa's sat up straight and blinked very fast, as if that would hide the tears. "That would be wonderful. I'll take a nap to make sure my strength lasts. Go to school now, and get your DPS test with your class, and remember that I will love you whatever happens."

Elena ran down the stairs, thumping all the way, with the

memory of Papa's smile like a small warm spot in her cold, aching heart.

The van was stuffy and smelled like sausage, and Mrs. Givens was yawning. Izzie was sitting way down in the bench seat with her boots up against her mother's seat back. She wrinkled her nose and stuck out her tongue, which was shorthand for: *watch out, Mom is having one of her bad mornings.*

Elena buckled up and said polite things, and soon they were picking up Kelli from her apartment complex.

"Honestly, girls," Mrs. Givens said as Kelli bounded down the outside steps. "What goes through your empty little heads? In ten years, you're going to look back at pictures of yourselves and die of embarrassment."

Izzie rolled her eyes. "Mom, please. We're the Trouble Triplets. We're supposed to look shocking."

Friday was No-Uniforms day, and there was a stupid choir assembly too, so they'd decided to pull out all the stops. That meant black and white horizontal striped shirts, vertically-striped tights, big black boots and little black skirts.

Everyone's hair was still in the matching tiny braids from last weekend's sleepover. Izzie's was coming loose, but the frazzled look worked with her perky nose. They were the same height since Kelli had grown an inch, and when they stood in a row they were as perfect as one of Papa's color swatches for earth tones. Kelli was deep mahogany brown, Elena tawny-gold, and Izzie pale fawn.

Izzy liked to say she was peachy, and they let her because making her happy was always easiest.

"I think we look outrageous," Elena said, because it was a great word.

Izzie echoed it, grinning. "Outraaaaaaaaaageous."

Mrs. Givens said, "You look ridiculous. Don't say I didn't tell you so."

Kelli didn't even mumble a hello. She slouched in the seat and slapped Izzie's arm when she got poked. "Stop it. I'm mad. And I can't go bowling tomorrow because I'm grounded, and I didn't even do anything."

Mrs. Givens laughed as she pulled onto the street. "Yes, you're a perfect little angel. All of you are. Kelli, I'll call your mom later and get the real story. Ellie, how is your dad doing? Is he all right?"

"Yes, he's fine. Oh. We're going out, tonight. Can Izzie come over to watch Marco and Teresa?"

After they made arrangements for babysitting, Mrs. Givens said, "And how's your mom?"

Elena bit her lip. "Fine. We had a video chat Wednesday." *She said my face is puffy, and that I buy too much junk food and meat. She doesn't say I'm fat and stupid, but I know she thinks it.* "She hates the desert."

"I hope she gets home for Marco's birthday. It's so hard on a toddler when a parent has to travel so much for work."

"That's the government for you," Kelli declared. "And stupid companies are worse. The military-industrial-super-corporations won't stop until they ruin the whole world with pollution and destroy us all, you'll see."

Mrs. Givens glared into the rear view mirror. "Kelli MacArthur, if you ever dirty my ears with your father's radical politics again, then you can find a new car pool. No wonder you're grounded. You called him again, didn't you?"

Kelli's lower lip trembled, and tears welled up in her eyes. "Yes, ma'am."

"Your mom cut off contact to protect you. I don't care if he was a big name with GlobalComm. He's disgraced and unemployed, and I don't blame your mom for divorcing him, not one bit. He'll be facing treason charges if he isn't careful. Don't let him drag you down with him. Do I make myself clear?"

"Yes, ma'am."

"Good."

Izzie mouthed an apology and made silly faces the rest of the way to school. Her cheeks were still bright red with embarrassment, and Kelli was still sniffling when they arrived right at the bell. Elena barely had time to sneak in supportive hugs before they had to split up and run to their first classes.

No one had a perfect life. Izzie's mom always knew better than anyone about everything, and Kelli's dad was a criminal. Elena supposed she was a horrible person for feeling better about herself because her best friends had problems too, but she did. And knowing someone understood even a little bit eased her fears. Together, they could face anything.

18 APRIL, 11:45 AM
SHERMAN MIDDLE SCHOOL, ELGIN, ILLINOIS

Elena's next chance to talk with her friends came during the long recess period while the first lunch group was in the cafeteria. She dodged past the boys who always loitered by the door to the gym, and then she stopped in her tracks.

A blond-haired young man in a gray DPS uniform was standing by the open door to the walk-around yard outside. He smiled and nodded politely, but Elena felt like crying at the sight of him.

Whenever she saw the uniforms, she saw Papa's rollover again. He'd cried and screamed so much, and she couldn't always stop the memories when they came. She ran behind the bleachers and crawled into the Trouble Triplet hidey hole they'd staked out there at the beginning of the school year.

She put her hands over her ears, closed her eyes and ignored everything until the screams in her head went away.

Kelli snuck in a few minutes later and dropped her book bag to the floor with a theatrical flourish. "What a day. Did you see all the dippies in the halls? I hate testing week."

Izzie arrived on her heels, saying, "I'm so glad I got mine done on Tuesday." Her braids were a complete mess now, and she brushed at the wavy blonde strands hanging in her face. "There's a dozen Marines from the Monster Brigade outside the dean's office. One of them has claws and striped fur like my cat. Did you two see them?"

"I didn't, no." Elena shook her head and tried to not think about blood and claws and Papa crying. She said, "But you shouldn't call them monsters, Izzie. It's mean. They're people like everyone else. Don't you ever see any of them at the market or downtown?"

"Ick, no. Not where we shop. My dad says he doesn't care how many jobs the base brings in, they're still eerie. That isn't mean, it's honest."

"That's what people say when they know they're being mean and don't want to fight about it," Kelli said. "But anyway, I didn't see them either. I went past the staff lounge and raided the vending machines. Look, treats for everyone."

She handed out chocolate bars from her backpack. Elena wanted to eat hers, but thought of calories and handed hers to Izzie while Kellie said, "I wonder why the Marines are here. Mercury Battalion doesn't do school visits."

Izzie said, "All the teachers tested Monday. Maybe one of them is about to roll. Remember the PSA from health class? What if it's a pyro, or some other elemental? Oh, or a troll!

One of the Marines is a troll. How exciting would it be to see one of them to hit onset right here at school?"

It would be the worst. The smell of the candy made Elena queasy. "You don't ever want to see onset for something big or physical. It isn't exciting. It's gross when someone goes through the change all in one hot session. I was scared to death when Papa rolled, and he's only a carnie with barely any power at all."

"Oh, Elena." Izzie's eyes went wide. "I'm sorry. I forgot. I didn't think."

"You're good at that," Kelli said. "Not thinking, I mean." Her eyes widened, and she snapped her fingers. "Hey, I think I know why the Marines are here. It's the last day of screenings. The Dips will be at all the exits checking IDs against the test lists, in case they missed anyone. The Marines are here to bully people into behaving, plus to chase down any runners. As if anyone would be that stupid."

Elena's face heated up. Her clever plan to sneak away at lunch never would have worked. Papa's lecture had saved her a lot of embarrassment.

Izzie licked her fingers clean. "What a huge fuss over nothing. It's only a blood test, and it's for our own good. Why would anyone skip it?"

The idea of facing the assessment without fear made Elena's brain spin. The idea of dismissing its importance made her want to punch Izzie in the face. She clenched her fists instead. "Did you get your results yet?"

"Oh, sure. Yesterday. I'm a null, of course. Everybody in my family is except for my cousin Emily. Her and her daughter, I guess. I wasn't worried."

How are you my friend? Elena wanted to scream. "It isn't genetic, Izzie. You know that. It was on the Health test we all aced. The screening tests are important because they're all we have. You *know* nobody knows why people hit onset or don't. I know you're smart. Why do you act so ignorant?"

Kelli added, "You're being selfish, too. Maybe you don't have to worry, but don't you care about anyone else? My homeroom tested yesterday, so I'm stuck waiting until Monday and I'm so nervous I can barely breathe. It's why I called Dad. Mom said she would disown me if I'm positive, and she meant it. It isn't fair. Anyone can test positive. Anyone can roll."

The passing bell rang, and the crowd in the gym headed for the cafeteria. Izzie licked each one of her fingers again like a contented little cat. "Yes, but everyone doesn't roll, do they? Only one in ten ever rolls hard enough to tell. That's less than half of the people who test positive. Some years only three or four percent roll. See? I do remember. I am not ignorant. Take it back. "

She and Kelli both looked at Elena.

Elena sighed. "I take it back."

And Izzie said, "I didn't mean to hurt your feelings, Kelli. I'm sure you'll be fine even if you are poz. Your mom loves you, right? Come on, TTs. Let's get in line for real lunch."

And with that, she led them along to the cafeteria the way she always did, bossy and confident in a way Elena envied.

At their usual table, Izzie chewed through a huge sub sandwich full of meat and juicy sauce, and Kelli bought a hot lunch that smelled heavenly. Elena made her meal last as long as possible, but it wasn't easy.

She was picking at the last crumbs of her cookie when Izzie said, "I don't think the dips would bring along all the monsters unless something's about to go wrong. And I *am* smart, and I *do* know how to think, so there."

Kelli said, "Nah, it's only a show of force: a reminder that the government can reach anyone. They want us scared. Terror tactics squash dissent and bully the population into compliance. That's how oppressors stay in power."

Izzie glared at her. "Seriously, Kelli? I'm not my mom, but could you quit with the radical stuff for once? This isn't political."

"Isn't it?" Elena said after thinking about it. "Isn't that what a show of force is, like we talked about in Civics? A pyro or a troll could kill everyone in the school, sure, but that could happen any day. Their job is to protect us all the time. Why be here today unless it's what Kelli's saying, that knowing they could squash people is a threat to make us all behave? I'm not saying it's right, just that it might be true."

Right and wrong weren't always easy to pin down. Her mother worked for the government now, bringing water to drought-stricken areas all over the world, but if that was the right way to solve the problem, then she wouldn't have to go away again and again.

Nothing in the world was perfect. In a perfect world, she would have two normal parents and a regular, ordinary life.

Izzie groaned. "Stop it, I'm begging you. Both of you make my head hurt. Let's talk about the assembly. Do you think they'll try to make us all sing again this year?"

That conversation occupied them until the bell rang for end of the second lunch shift. The PA system issued the reminder that due to the assembly, all students should return to their homerooms, not their regular afternoon classes, finishing with, "—except for Homerooms 6 and 12, who will report to Dean Fratelli's office."

Elena had to swallow a bunch of times to keep her lunch down. "Well, that's me."

Her friends both stared at her. Izzie blinked first. "Oh, Ellie, you goose. I completely forgot you hadn't tested yet. Are you petrified? You are, aren't you? I should've been lots nicer. Say you forgive me, or I will die. I'll ask mom to let us have a sleepover Sunday, to keep you two from worrying yourselves to death all alone at home. Please say you'll come. Triplets together, right?"

"You're the goose," Elena said. Tears welled up in her eyes, but a smile rose with them, and she felt warm all over. *This is why we're friends.* "That will be tons of fun. I'll beg Papa to say yes. I'm sure he will. TTs forever."

They hooked pinkie fingers and shook on the promise.

Dean Fratelli was directing traffic in the wide main corridor outside the administration center, lining up students along the lockers near the hall door to his office. Only two Marines were visible through the glass doors of the main office, not a dozen.

One of them did have striped fur, and his eyes were big and pale like Papa's. The other man had on mirrored sunglasses, and he was bigger than anyone Elena had ever seen.

They both wore funny hats, crisp khaki shirts, and big webbed belts with pistols in holsters. The secretaries behind the front counter were chatting fearlessly with them.

Izzie ran off after delivering a big bouncing hug. Kelli gave the two Marines a long, frowning look, then offered Elena a souvenir penny embossed with a paw print logo from the zoo. "For luck," she said. "I don't believe in luck, but Mom gave it to me. Pass it on, when you're done."

Elena squeezed it hard. The fear didn't go away, but the gesture helped.

18 APRIL, 12:55 PM
SHERMAN MIDDLE SCHOOL, ELGIN, ILLINOIS

The test wasn't scary at all. Standing in the hall while all the other classes marched to the auditorium was the worst part. She went into the office when her name was called, and the Public Safety aide filled up a little tube with blood.

"All done," the aide said while she taped a cotton ball over Elena's skin and bent her arm up. "There you go. Good as new."

The knot of fear in Elena's stomach loosened. She still didn't want to know the results, but it was out of her hands now. All she could do was wait and pray.

The aide attached a label to the blood-filled vial. When Elena straightened her elbow, blood trickled down her forearm.

The aide said, "Hm. That won't do." She removed the bandage and stroked a finger over the dark, swollen lump around the needle mark. Tingling warmth slithered down Elena's arm, and the bruise disappeared. The aide smiled. "That's better."

Elena wiggled her fingers. *If I have to roll, I wouldn't mind a power like that. Something small and helpful. That's something I can pray for, tonight at church.* She peeked at the name badge on the aide's white lab coat. "That is neat. Thank you, Ms. Watkins."

"You're welcome." The aide's hair was white and fluffy, and her skin was the same color and wrinkled texture as a dried apple slice. It crinkled around her dark brown eyes when she smiled again. "I can't do that for everyone, but I'm allowed to make exceptions. I'll note it for the school nurse. How are you feeling?"

"Why?" Elena's stomach started to ache again. "Am I sick?"

"Nothing that a few supplements won't cure." Ms. Watkins stopped smiling. "Listen, dear. Dispensing wisdom is one of the few perks that comes with being old. I'm sure you'll ignore it, but I can't help trying. Are you listening?"

Elena prepared herself for a lecture. "Sure, whatever."

"I believed in all kinds of superstitions when I was your age. My uncle died in rollover, you see, and I tested factor-plus with very high numbers. Of course I looked for a way to beat the odds."

"There isn't one," Elena said dutifully. All the lessons said that, but maybe the lessons were wrong. Weren't scientists always discovering new things?

Ms. Watkins took Elena's hand, turning it over and pressing it between her soft palms. "You say the words, but do you believe them? I know children whisper the same stories, year after year. Earlier this week, a girl asked if I was infecting her with the test, and that idiotic conspiracy theory went underground in the fifties. You hear a rumor, read a book someone shows you, and you think *maybe*. You think, *it can't hurt.*"

Elena met the woman's eyes and lied. "I don't know what you mean."

"Yes, you do. You're anemic and underweight. Starving yourself through puberty won't affect your blood factor status. That fairy tale has been around forever. It's a lie. Stupid girls starve themselves to death."

I'm not stupid. I'm scared. Elena didn't admit that. If she spoke, she would cry.

Ms. Watkins patted Elena's hand. "There now. You seem like a smart girl, so that's all the nagging I'll do. If you have any other questions, you're welcome to chat with the outreach team from Mercury Battalion, and you can make an appointment through them to talk to a DPS counselor privately, too. That's with or without your parents. It's why the soldiers are here: to listen, and to help."

So much for Kelli's theory. The Marines were not here as a show of force, they were doing community service. Elena pictured the pair in the office again. Her spirits rose. "I can ask them anything?"

Ms. Watkins pursed her lips. "If you ask Sergeant Coby if he's a real troll, you'll get a lecture on history and mythology. I wouldn't recommend it."

"I would never." Elena couldn't even imagine being that horrid. "But the other one is a C-N combo, isn't he? Probably a one or a two, since he's in Mercury."

"Corporal Tillman is a N2C, that's right. You know your designations. Are you a monster buff, then?" Ms. Watkins sounded disappointed.

"No, but my baby brother has a big book of charts that he likes me to read at bedtime. Knowing more helps him adjust, the therapist said. See, our papa hit onset a few months ago, and now he's a C9N, so I wanted to ask the soldier how —he—um."

There was no good way to say it. Elena's face heated. "Papa sheds now. He only has a ruff on his neck and back, but it gets everywhere in the laundry. Would it be rude to ask the corporal how he gets the fur out of his shirt collars?"

Ms. Watkins blinked several times, and then she smiled. "That question might make Tillman's whole day. Please do ask. Ask Sergeant Coby about scales, too. I hear they're equally hard on clothes." She pointed at the main office door. "Now, scoot along and send in the next student."

18 APRIL, 1:15 PM
SHERMAN MIDDLE SCHOOL, ELGIN, ILLINOIS.

Corporal Tillman answered Elena's questions in great detail. He didn't hide his fangs when he smiled, but Elena made herself smile back.

The rest of the testing finished up while they were talking. Huge Sergeant Coby fielded a few questions from other students as they came out of the nurse's office, but most of them went on their way to the assembly with their eyes down and feet moving fast.

Melissa Reardon was the last student out. She took one look at the Marines and bolted into the hall at a dead run.

Her form was awful. Coach Gibbs would make her do extra laps for the flappy hands. Tillman paused in the act of handing Elena a card with his contact information on it to watch Melissa's exit. "Damn, Sarge. Just like you predicted. Are you always right?"

"Watch your language, Corporal," Sergeant Coby said. His voice was low and rumbly, and it made his words sound sad, like Papa's lisp. "And yes, I can tell the rabbits from the tigers a mile away."

He glanced at an electronic clipboard that looked tiny in his hands, and then he tapped the radio microphone on his uniform collar. "Lieutenant, the flock is sheared. Ms. Watkins is ready for escort. We're wrapping up Q and A." After a pause, he nodded. "Aye, aye, sir. Backup on out-routes from the dog and pony show. I copy four short, and I have the photo list. Wait one. I'll confirm handoff."

Coby opened the door to the office and bent to peer inside. Elena watched the man's broad back while he spoke to the nurse. His muscles bulged, pressing his armored skin against the uniform shirt in ridges a little like a turtle's shell.

His appearance didn't bother Elena half as much as her father's did. Even Tillman had been more interesting than frightening once she got used to the pointy-toothed smile. She wondered why it was so different. *Maybe it's because they were never my Papa.*

The sergeant kept his hands curled to hide the thick nails, but from his size, he was at least a T5. The hardened plating on his skin wasn't noticeable until you looked for the edges, though, and the tinted glasses might mean he was light sensitive. That would make him a rare Y variant. Marco would be thrilled to put a new checkmark on their spotting list.

Coby smiled as he turned back to Elena. His teeth were all very sharp like Tillman's. He said, "You're still here, little tiger? You'll miss the start of the assembly."

Run, fear whispered. Elena curled her toes in her shoes. *No.* "I had another question. For you. Ms. Watkins said I should ask how you get scale off your clothes."

"Oh, did she?" Coby aimed a frown at Corporal Tillman.

He raised both hands, claws out. "I didn't say a word, I swear. Glass houses, man. A guy who has to bleach venom stains out of his socks never casts the first laundry stone."

Dean Fratelli looked in from the hallway. "Sergeant, I don't want to rush you, but I'm needed in the auditorium."

"Go ahead, sir. We're right behind you." The sergeant gave Elena another smile. "I'll make you a deal, little tiger. If you'll walk with us to our post outside the auditorium, I'll tell you all about my lesson in the power of chemistry on the way. Fair trade?"

He offered his hand. Elena looked at the sharp, thick nails, then leaned back and saw her tiny reflections in the man's glasses. She clasped his fingers. His grip was warm and gentle. "Deal," she said.

The hallways were always eerie when the school was empty. The addition that held the auditorium and the vocational workshops was attached to the main building by a single corridor on the first floor. High windows at both ends of the central hall cast bright rectangles of spring sunshine down the center of the main hall, and light pooled on the scuffed tile floor.

Sergeant Coby kept to the shadows, and he walked slowly while he told his story.

Back when he'd first rolled, he'd been instructed to presoak his wash in vinegar. It dissolved flaked bits of armor out of the seams so they wouldn't wear through as fast.

He tried to save time by adding soda and soap without draining the machine first.

Elena had done that experiment in sixth grade science. She pictured the massive sergeant standing at a clogged washer in a huge pile of sudsy bubbles, and she couldn't help giggling. Corporal Tillman laughed too, and echoes bounced off the lockers all along the empty hall.

Elena remembered that detail for a long time afterwards: the corporal was laughing when he turned the corner.

Light flared.

Coby scooped Elena up and clasped her against his hard chest, and she shrieked at the top of her lungs until the floor knocked the wind out of her. The sergeant's weight felt as heavy as the world on her back. Sunglasses and a hat landed in front of her nose. Glass and bricks pinged and clashed and smashed to the floor everywhere.

Firecrackers popped in the distance, and people were screaming, and she couldn't breathe. Then the sergeant was

flinch. He rolled his shoulder and frowned at her. "You going to start bawling again, tiger?"

"No." Tears stung her eyes, but she scrunched up her face as fiercely as she could. "Not if you tell me what happened."

Coby snorted. "What happened is that somebody out there blew up a truck and every piece of school property that had a Marine standing near it. Don't panic, your classmates and teachers are all safe for now. We told them the assembly was —never mind. I'll get you there safe. Don't run ahead. Wait for me, got it?"

"No! I don't get anything. How can you be so calm? Did you know this was going to happen? Why didn't you stop it? Why would anyone want to hurt us?"

All the questions came bursting out so fast that Elena had to bite her tongue to stop them. Coby wasn't going to answer. He wasn't even looking at her. He was helping his friend.

Tillman moaned when the sergeant lifted him. His eyes were shut, but his fangs were out, and glistening droplets hung from the tips of his fangs and fingertips. Elena shrank away when Coby swung around with him.

The sergeant said, "Stay on my left, tiger. Left side only, understand?"

Elena nodded. If she stayed on that side, his body would be between her and the hole in the wall.

The battered fire doors wouldn't open. Coby knocked one off its hinges with two sharp kicks. The metal panel clanged to the floor. The narrow lobby beyond it was empty and dark. The exit doors to the front sidewalk lay on the floor in blasted pieces, but the outside security shutters had come down in their place.

Coby paused at the first set of closed auditorium doors. "Tillman, you still with me?"

"Wha—?"

"Listen up. Looks like those crank calls to the principal were legit. Someone with rockets or pyro support took out the DPS unit and most of our team. I'm ordered to secure the site until backup drops in. I'm going to have to leave you with the dips and the civilians. Don't you dare spike anyb—"

"You've seen our power!"

The amplified voice from outside drowned out Coby's voice. He had Tillman on the floor and his pistol aimed at the hallway behind them a second later. Elena scurried behind him.

The man outside said, "Now hear our truth. The Department of Public Safety was created to control us, not to protect us. The government blackmails us with our futures, silences dissent with disease, and crushes opposition with brute force. Internment and reeducation elevate the unworthy and oppress those who worked hard for success. We will no longer stand aside and let the government destroy our lives. The monsters must die, and the system with them. The revolution starts today. It starts here."

When the voice went silent, sirens became audible.

Elena felt dizzy. She had never heard anything so crazy in her life, but she knew the voice. That nasal drone had put her to sleep in every French class her first semester in seventh grade. The teacher had left at mid-term. She couldn't remember why.

She asked, "What is Mr. Hall doing here?"

"Committing treason," the sergeant said, and relayed the name to someone over the radio.

A squeal of feedback preceded Mr. Hall's next words. "It's time to pick a side. If you shelter the enemy, you are the enemy. Send out the monsters and their makers, or die with them. We want our children to live free, but we will not shrink from sacrifice. You have five minutes."

Coby made a noise that was so deep that Elena felt it in her bones more than she heard it. The hair on her arms rose, and prickles ran up her spine.

"What do we do now?" she asked, because she couldn't bear to listen to that growling in silence. The sound stopped, and Coby showed his teeth. It wasn't a smile. Dogs bared their fangs like that before they fought, and so did baboons at the zoo.

"Now I make sure your teachers do the right thing," he said.

18 APRIL, 1:35 PM
SHERMAN MIDDLE SCHOOL ANNEX, ELGIN, ILLINOIS

Sergeant Coby slammed open the door into the auditorium with his shoulder, and the roar of three hundred people talking at once spilled over Elena in a solid wave of sound. When the sergeant shouted, "Marines, on me, now," the words bounced off the walls into a shocked silence. He added in the same carrying, commanding tone, "Bring the dips with you. Everyone else, out of the way."

A group of teachers in the aisle scattered to seats at the ends of rows, and the noise rose again. On the stage at the far end of the room, Principal Hogan grabbed the microphone stand in front of the empty choir risers. It scraped over the boards, and a piercing hum rose over the babble.

"Remain seated," she said, and her voice was like the sergeant's, sharp and full of authority. "Quiet, please. Everything is going to be fine."

The principal sounded convincing, but that had to be the

LOCKDOWN   167

biggest lie Elena had ever heard. She checked the usual row in back for Kelli and Izzie. They were easy to spot in their black and white stripes. Izzie's nose was red and her eyes were puffy. Kelli's mouth was moving. She pointed at a seat.

If Elena sat down, she would start to scream and never stop. She pointed at herself, meaning *no, you come here.* Kelli shoved Izzie, and they started swapping seats with other students to get closer.

Mr. Fratelli came hustling up the aisle, huffing and red-faced. His hair wisped over his bald spot and his belly jiggled, and on any other day, Elena would have been howling with laughter. Now she wanted to cry, because the reason the dean was out of breath was that he was doing most of the walking for a woman in bloodstained khaki who could barely stay on her feet.

Over in the far aisle, three people in gray DPS uniforms were helping a bloody, scaled figure limp towards the doors on that side. Mr. Fratelli said, "You can't be serious, Sergeant. You can't go out there. You're supposed to be protecting us."

"I am," Coby said. "If we stay, that nut will bring down the building and tell the world you were afraid to force us out. If we go, he'll might blow the building anyway and say we did it, but probably not because that'd be a provable lie. Worst case, you and Principal Hogan gain time for evac. Best case, we'll hold him until the Marines bring down the wrath of God on his ass. Either way, this terrorist does not get the live-feed imagery of callous government brutality that he wants. Go. Now."

Mr. Fratelli gave Izzie a puzzled glance as she arrived at the aisle seat, but then he hurried back to the stage. The woman Marine had weird eyes, white all the way around the dots of her pupils. She said, "I'm tapped out, Sarge, and the blast got most of Marin's tail and part of his left foot. Won't be much of a scuffle."

"Won't need to be." Coby pointed to the group on the other side of the auditorium, then to the lobby, before putting his arm around his comrade's shoulders and retreating with her. "All we have to do—"

The door shut on his words.

Elena could not stop trembling. Izzie jumped out of her seat and tried to squeeze her to death. "Did you hear him? Mr. Hall?" She sniffled. "He's friends with Mom and Dad, and he was at my house last night, can you believe it? Mom made pancakes for dinner, my favorite, after we got my test result, and Dad didn't even yell about it because I said it was a mistake, I must be a null, and he said so, but now—and now—do you think they knew this would happen today?"

Elena's heart broke, but she didn't know what words to say. She met Kelli's eyes, and they both hugged Izzie as if the world was ending, because in a way it had for Izzie, and it might being ending for all of them soon.

"Attention, everyone," Principal Hogan said. "I know you're frightened, but stay calm, and we'll be fine. We're going to do a fire drill, up and out the back of the stage here. File out like we've practiced—"

Elena stopped listening. It was all lies, and she knew it. Anyone with eyes could see the place was packed. No one in the rear of the auditorium would get to the front in time.

Mr. Hall had blown up kind, old Ms. Watkins, and the smiling man from the gym, and a whole lot of other people, and now he was going to blow up everyone else because he hated some of them for things they couldn't change.

A quiet thought rose up: *if you have to die, wouldn't you rather die with the people who tried to save you?*

Elena turned away from the crowd, and eased open the lobby door. It swung wide as Kelli pushed harder, behind her.

"Trouble Triplets," she said when Elena frowned at her, and Izzie nodded, sniffling. "Together, Elena. We go together."

Elena took her hand, and Izzie took Kelly's.

The Marines had taken off their belts, weapons and uniform tops. The woman's undershirt had been white once. Now it was splotched with dark red. The scaled man had a bloody stump of a tail, and two men in white dress shirts and gray trousers were helping him balance. The third DPS employee, an older woman, was wrapping her uniform blazer around the bar still sticking out of Tillman.

Coby picked up the corporal as if he weighed nothing and moved him into the crook of one arm. "They probably won't blast us until we're in the clear, nice and visible. Forward in rank as soon as the shutters lift. Make sure they see you, then fall in behind me if you can. Five minutes is our—"

He stared at Elena. "Where the fuck do you think you're going, tiger?"

Kelli giggled at the obscenity, and Izzie gasped. Elena lifted her chin and looked all the way up. The sergeant looked terrifying, and he sounded worse, but he had soft, kind eyes behind those glasses. Elena raised her free hand and hooked her fingers into his. "We're coming with you."

22 APRIL 09:15S
USMC CAMP BUTLER, ELGIN ILLINOIS.

Captain Malik Jefferson swiped the imagery from his desk screen to the larger display on the wall behind him. He made the gesture with more force than strictly necessary, but he'd earned the right to some aggravation. After four straight days of damage control meetings, press conferences, report-writing and political spin, he was more than ready to let a little of the emotional overload roll downhill.

"Look at this," he said to the soldier standing at stiff attention in front of his desk. "Look at it, Jackass. This picture is still a top hit on every news outlet in the country a week after it was taken. Holding the record for early onset lifespan wasn't enough for you? You had to get a little more publicity, did you?"

"No, sir." Sergeant Coby's service uniform was recruiting-poster perfection from the top of his cover to the toes of his shiny black boots, and his posture was regulation precise in every degree.

Between the reflective glasses and the limited mobility of his facial muscles, his expression was more than honor-guard blank. It was unreadable. The tone, though—his voice always gave him away. He was worried.

Captain Jefferson stopped teasing him and turned in his chair to inspect the photographs for himself. Coby had come a long way in the six months since Jefferson had taken command of Camp Butler, but he still struggled with interactions outside the chain of command. He did have a sense of humor; he simply never applied it to his job.

The image was pixelated from magnification, but it glowed bright in the dim room. Sergeant Coby was the centerpiece, out of uniform, bloodstained and looking even grimmer than he did today. Cameras exposed the telltale glow of incipient rampage a null's eyes never saw, and the photographer had a magnificent eye for light and shadow. He'd even captured the sense of musculature swelling larger beneath armored skin.

The gentleness of Coby's clawed grip on the limp, bloody

man in his arms made a brilliant counterpoint to the show of physical strength. Beside him in the image, Corporal Meredith Fergus was ethereal and unearthly, her own aura faint and her eyes opaque with fatigue. Private Angelo Marin on her far side looked like a defeated dragon. The array of men and woman framing them— equally battered, identically determined—offset the unarmed rollover Marines with perfect, vulnerable humanity.

The foreground provided the crowning touch which had made the image an instant international sensation and a shoo-in for the year's Pulitzer award: three young women with tear-streaked faces. They were dressed in stark black and white, and the one with the calm smile of a saint was holding the biggest monster of all by the hand, leading him out of the shadows into the sunshine.

"You're a goddamned Jesus at the Last Supper with a touch of the Pieta and all the little children thrown in for good measure," Jefferson said. "Looks like you paid attention to all those psy-ops classes you thought no one knew you audited. Surrendering like that was a brilliant propaganda stunt. I have only one question: did you expect to survive it?"

Sergeant Coby's chin rose slightly. "I had two hundred and ninety four children and fifty-plus civilian adults in retreat. The best I could do was offer a distraction and spike the opposition's propaganda machine as conspicuously as possible."

"That is not an answer, sergeant. What possessed you to add three children to the distraction?"

"Sir, I didn't—and she—I—" Coby fumbled to a halt. "Have you met her, sir?"

"Elena Moreno? Yes." Jefferson savored the memory for a few seconds. "I sat in on her debrief. She says she going to study politics and law so she can get elected to Congress. And she's trading in her extra-curricular athletics for internship with DPS. She has nerves of steel and a sharp mind behind that sweet face. Give her ten years and some training, and she might actually change the world."

"Well, sir, it was her idea, and I didn't have time to argue with her."

Jefferson nodded. "I understand. But the result was so perfect I've been accused of staging the whole incident. I am happy that the opposition was so busy arguing over the impact of martyring you that we captured them without further losses, but that's no excuse doing it in the first place. What kind of punishment do you think would be appropriate for endangering children, Staff Sergeant?"

"Sir, I told her to stay—" Coby stopped cold again. "Sir? Did you say Staff Sergeant, sir?"

He seriously had thought he was about to be reprimanded. Jefferson stood up and held out a hand. "I did. Congratulations, Staff. You saved lives at the risk of your own, and I'm proud of you. The promotion is only a temporary bump though, so don't get used to it."

"Sir, I'm—" Coby paused after shaking hands and tried again. "I don't understand, sir. Temporary?"

"You can't be an officer *and* a non-com, can you? Didn't I mention that you're applying for OCS? My aide has the papers all ready for your signature." Jefferson allowed himself a smile, saw the expression reflected in the sergeant's sunglasses and grinned wider. "At ease, Staff. Ask your questions."

Coby relaxed to parade rest, and his jaw worked sideways. "Why bother, sir? You know the odds of me living long enough to get through OCS? I'm weeks into that age record."

"Long odds, indeed." Jefferson pretended to give the objection some thought before shrugging. "You faced longer ones last week, and here you are. I'll bet on you again. Besides, like it or not, you're the Company's shiny public face right now, and shiny faces get shiny jobs. Since I can't have less than a lieutenant as a DPS liaison, Lieutenant Coby you shall be."

The mutter of voices in the outer office sounded loud in the silence that met his words.

He added gently, "Your next line is, *thank you, sir.*"

Coby nodded. "Thank you for the opportunity, sir. And I mean that. Not for the dip job, but for the vote of confidence."

"You've earned it." Jefferson sat down and made a show of picking up his pen. "You're dismissed until tomorrow at oh-nine-hundred, when you will report to the local DPS office. You'll be going through orientation with the new crop of interns."

That news brought Coby's chin up. Suspicion colored his voice when he said, "Interns, sir? You mentioned earlier—is Elena Moreno one of them?"

"Of course she is." Jefferson made a supreme effort to keep a straight face. "Sometimes politics stinks, but sometimes a little good comes out of it. I cannot wait to read about the headaches the pair of you will cause DPS administration just by being yourselves. For now, dismissed means go away, in case you've forgotten."

The staff sergeant was still shaking his head on his way out the door.

Jefferson chuckled under his breath and got back to his paperwork. Some days he really enjoyed his job.

INTERVIEW WITH A HERO

INTERIOR: a television talk show set.

The STAGE is spot-lit at "intimate conversation" levels.
Seated AUDIENCE is visible only as dim figures against a
back wall decorated with uplights.

THE PLAYERS:

BRIAN GRIMM, wearing black eyeglasses, sitting in an
easy chair grinning ear to ear. Blond hair in a spiky moussed
cut, heavy beige face makeup, gym-lean body clad in double-
breasted dark pinstripes. He holds a stack of pale yellow notecards, which he regularly shuffles and rearranges. He looks
like a child next to the man sitting on the heavy steel bench
opposite him.

JACK COBY, a giant dressed in a crisply-starched white
dress shirt and black dress trousers, seated on a sturdy
METAL BENCH with visible rivets. Ordinary clothes cannot
disguise his eight-foot height or his stiff, thick skin. He is
sporting a black baseball cap and mirrored sunglasses, and he,

too, has a case of the fidgets, drumming the fingers of both hands against his legs.

Perky theme music swells and fades. Lights on the audience brighten.

BRIAN:
Welcome to the Brian Grimm show, everyone! I'm Brian Grimm, but of course you all know that.

Brian leans forward towards his guest while audience laughs.

BRIAN:
Hi, there. You're my biggest interview ever, you know that?

Camera cuts to show audience laughing, then returns to show both men on the stage.

BRIAN:
What should I call you? I'm not very knowledgeable about the military. Ranks and all that. I want to get it right.

JACK:
You can call me Jack.

BRIAN:
Oh, please. Come at me with the whole deal. Name, what you do, all of it. My viewers like to get all the juicy details.

Jack shifts his weight back, shoulders straightening. The metal bench creaks. He folds his arms.

JACK:

Full name and rank? Jack Coby, lieutenant, retired, United States Marine Corps. Gateway Company, Mercury Battalion. I work for the Department of Public Safety now. Not a lot of employment opportunities for an eight-foot tall armor-plated dude. I don't think you need my serial number on top of all that, do you?

BRIAN:

No, that is quite complicated enough. So is it Jack like Jack and the Beanstalk, only you're the giant?

Brian pauses for more audience reaction, mugs for the camera. Audience responds with nervous giggles.

Jack shrugs without answering. He resumes drumming his hands on his thighs.

BRIAN (patiently):

What I meant was, Jack is usually a nickname for something else.

JACK:

Oh! No, I'm not John or Jackson or anything else. My only nickname…can I say Jackass on TV? That's the only other thing people call me.

BRIAN:

I wouldn't dare! I was delighted when the Department approached my producers about having you on the show, but I confess you are one scary fellow. Will you tell us more about your powers? What's it like, being what you are?

JACK:

That's kinda personal. It's funny, which people always ask
that one. Getting nervous, are you? Didn't I read somewhere
you test positive for R-factor yourself?

Brian squirms, clears his throat, shuffles notecards.

BRIAN:

Ah—yes, it's true. Someone leaked my medical records.
Hazard of being a celebrity. I haven't rolled, though. Not yet. I
didn't mean to be insensitive. You don't have to answer, of
course.

Brian gives his guest a weak but earnest smile.

JACK:

Don't I? Isn't that why I'm here? To answer questions? That
sure sounded like a soft-pitch so I could reassure you that
you'll still be human even if you end up like me. Is that what
you want to hear?

BRIAN:

Errm. Maybe?

Camera cuts to various reactions from the audience.

BRIAN:

I confess I have my moments, wondering what's going to
happen to me when I get older.

Jack smiles wide enough to show large, curving, sharp canine
teeth. The smile does not look friendly.

JACK:

Relax, man. You'll probably never transition from latent to
active. Most poz don't. Less than fice percent of the overall
population last year, if I remember right. Ten percent overall.
Even if you do roll, you probably won't end up like me. T's,
P's, and R's are super rare. And Tee's are the most extreme.

Brian straightens, then leans forward with an intense
expression.

BRIAN:

Which brings us back to my question. What *is* it like, since
you don't mind sharing? Are you typical? I'm told you're
pretty rare even for a Tee.

JACK:

Yes and no. I'm T5, in the middle for power, with a Y-variant,
so I still look mostly human. Minimal armoring, no horns or
major spines, and claws not much longer than fingernails. I'm
also photosensitive, so I'd appreciate the camera light aiming
a little higher, thanks. The prime Tees are twelve feet tall at
baseline, and bigger yet in rampage high-power mode.

Stock video imagery comes up on the rear walls of the set,
showing cut shots of troops advancing on a jungle position,
with uniformed giants marching alongside armored vehicles
and normal-sized infantry.

JACK:

Oh, hey. That was an exercise in Hawaii. I remember that. I'm
the little guy there by the rightmost troop carrier. See the
difference? I'm only big and have the turtle-skin. Oh, and

we're all nearly impossible to kill between the armor and the regeneration. But the thing that makes me rare? I hit rollover at fourteen instead of forty or older like most people. Only ever been a couple of early onset Tees who survived rollover. That's what most people obsess about.

BRIAN:
Understandable! Fourteen. Wow. When the average rollover age is forty-seven? Remarkable. That must have been such a shock. Your family, how did they handle it?

JACK:
Don't know. Haven't seen my mom since I rolled. Something about me being a murderer and a monster and all that.

Brian boggles, eyes wide, mouth dropping open.

Jack sighs. Heavily.

JACK:
There's no way you didn't know that, but fine. I agreed to be on the show, this is outreach, so here's the story. I had a big brother. He's one of four people I killed during rollover, when the first rampage hit and I was out of my mind, disoriented and clumsy. I got a choice: execution or redemption in service. I chose to put on the uniform and swore the oath.

BRIAN:
That must have been…no. I honestly can't imagine. Thank you for sharing that. You are an astonishing young man. Now, about rampage mode. That's unique to Tee's, correct? How does it work? Can you demonstrate for us?

JACK:

Do you have something handy for me to demolish? No? Okay,
then. No rampage. If I call up the energy, I have to expend it
somehow. It isn't a rage thing. Couldn't be good soldiers if we
were always going crazy, could we? It isn't unique to Tee's,
either. It shows up as a variant in a bunch of other series.
Uncontrolled emotion makes anybody dangerous. There's a
feedback loop for us. Fight-or-flight impulses can trigger a
power burst and increase in abilities. A lot of variables can
bring it on. Rampage mode is just one more power we learn
to control and channel.

BRIAN:

And you control it marvelously. Speaking of soldiering…you
certainly had a busy time while you were in uniform. Maybe
you'll tell us a little about that? And you hold the world
record for age past rollover, too, don't you?

JACK:

Oh, heck, no. Alice Akiyama is the record-holder. She was in
her sixties when she rolled on First Night, back in '43, and
she hasn't aged a day since. She's a hundred something. But
for early onset cases? Yeah. I break that record every day I
wake up. No big deal.

BRIAN:

No big de—how can you be so calm about it? Nothing shakes
you, does it? I'm in awe, honestly. The Crisis Night incident,
the Elgin School bombings, the Gulf rescues…

New images come up on the set walls and flash by one after another–clips of text headlines, running children, walls of flame, uniformed soldiers and police officers, blanket-covered lumps in rubble, smoking craters, crowds holding hands…

BRIAN:
Look at all that. You and your unit, they saved so many lives.
Your bravery is just mind-boggling.

JACK:
I do seem to end up in the thick of things a lot, don't I? I never feel brave. I volunteered for most of those missions. My CO said it's an early onset thing. He says because we know we won't be around for long, we either go in hard or check out. Mostly I feel like I'm a regular guy. Dying young? That's the straw I drew. Getting upset wouldn't change it. I like to have some fun, have a few drinks, goof off. You know, regular stuff.

BRIAN:
So would you say you're someone who can handle pressure?

JACK:
Pressure? Sure, I can handle it. Oh—you're fishing for a story again, aren't you? My interview coach told me you people like stories. Okay, how about this thing my Mercury squad handled a few days before Crisis Night, what, a year ago or more now? It's the kind of thing Mercury Battalion handles ten, twelve times a year, all over the country. No privacy violations, I won't name names or places.

Brian sets down his notecards, rubs his hands together.

BRIAN:
This sounds good already. Go on, do.

JACK:
Okay. This lady, she and her whole family were members of
some Denial group. She refused to report to internment camp
when her R-factor spiked, and she started rolling hot at
home. Worse, you know how one house in every block is the
one where all the kids go? Her place.

Jack pulls off his sunglasses and squints at audience for a
moment before putting the glasses back on.

JACK:
You all know what hot means, right? Someone rolls from poz
to active in hours, not weeks or months? It can get gruesome
when there are physical changes or elemental powers
involved. She rolled full-on pyro. Prime pyro. P-1A's like that
—back on First Night those were the kind of rollovers that
left Saint Louis and Spokane in ashes. And from the time a
new pyro starts glowing and showing, it's maybe an hour to
full uncontrolled ignition.

BRIAN:
Oooh, I can't even imagine.

Brian looks up and over his shoulder, speaks to someone off-
stage.

BRIAN:
Do we have pyro stock footage? Can we roll that?

The back of the set lights up with images of people inciner-
ating buildings, trees, and bushes, melting steel beams,
causing explosions.

Jack turns and looks over the top of the sunglasses to watch
the images as he continues speaking.

JACK:
Yeah. Like that. The lady's kids called their Dad. One of the
neighbor kids ran home, told his mom, and she called the
Department of Public Safety. The DPS scrambled a Mercury
team for containment. Dad was driving off with Mom when
the primary team teleported in. I do not know where the man
thought he was going. Deniers. Who can figure? Panic.
Anyway. The primaries weren't in position to pursue, not
with a burning house and a horde of kids right there to
contain. My squad gets teleported on-scene expecting to be
back-up, but there I am with a car driving off and smoke
billowing out, neighbors screaming and getting in the way,
and who knows how long before the whole block, maybe the
whole town goes up in a firestorm.

BRIAN:
Brr. Wow.

JACK:
Yeah. Now that, that was a high-pressure situation, but it's all
about keeping your head. There's a standard procedure,
believe it or not. I called the play, Corporal Amy Goodall--
she's a sergeant now, but she was a Corporal then—she
picked me up and launched me after the car. I was the
smallest Tee in the squad, she's the largest, twelve foot plus,

no big deal, right? I land on the car roof, it crumples and entraps, my 'porter sends me and it to the secured containment block back on base, and containment techs pulled the dad and me from the cell before the mom ignited. Boom, major crisis averted.

BRIAN:
How close was it?

JACK:
Ten seconds. She melted the containment block ten seconds after she got there. Any hesitation from us, and she would've leveled several blocks and killed hundreds of people. I guess she did good, once she got with the program. She ended up in reboot camp for Mercury once she got minimum control of course. Talent like that always goes through the military first.

BRIAN:
Not everyone gets that lucky or does so well, afterwards. How do you feel about the public anger directed towards the government's Public Safety policies?

JACK:
I was a Marine, and now I work for the Department of Public Safety. It's not my place to have feelings about policies. I go where I'm ordered. Mercury Battalion is a specialist unit, they handle the R-factor breakouts and containment and do a lot of R-null population outreach with the DPS, but we're soldiers first. Bottom line, all enemies of the United States, foreign and domestic, they're my business.

Brian turns to the cameras to display exaggerated surprise and disappointment. Everyone on the audience groans in unison, and Brian shakes his head at Jack.

BRIAN:
Seriously, Jack? You're going to feed me the official line and nothing else? Throw me a bone. Tell me how you really feel.

JACK:
No.

After a pause, Brian puts on the earnest smile again and waves off the uncomfortable moment with a flamboyant gesture.

BRIAN:
Fine, fine. Never mind. We're running low on time. I'll give you an easy one. Suppose you could wish for any power you wanted, change any one thing about yourself...

JACK:
That's a joke, right? Look at me. You think I wouldn't rather be normal size, lead a normal life? You think I wouldn't rather live longer than–hell, do I even know if I'll wake up tomorrow morning? What do you think I would pick? I would wish to be for plain old regular human, null-factor, no chance of rolling over. That'd mean I would have a chance of seeing twenty-five, maybe even getting married and have kids or something someday.

BRIAN:

That was…honest. Brutally honest, to be fair. There I was thinking you'd toss off a joke or tell me which power could possibly be better than yours.

A smattering of applause and nervous laughter from the audience.

JACK:

Oh, well. That's easy. If I had my pick of powers, then I'd love to be a 'porter. One of the variants that only needs a visual aid for a targeting reference. Traveling the world whenever I was off-duty, that would be pretty keen.

BRIAN:

That does sound fun. Now here's one question I ask all my guests. Will you tell us a secret?

JACK:

No. If I told you, it wouldn't be a secret, would it?

He grins again, flashing fewer teeth this time, and the audience response with laughter and another, stronger patter of applause. Brian waits for the noise to quiet.

BRIAN:

Well, that was a nice answer, and we're almost to the end of our time. Jack, you've been a good sport about all this. Really great. Can I throw one more at you? You can say no again if you don't want, but the one audience request that scores highest on every poll is this one: what's your biggest fear?

JACK:

Oh, that one I don't mind at all. I have two big fears. First, look at me. I can bench-press a pickup truck, and I'm bigger than two bulls stacked on top of each other. I'm afraid I'll hurt someone innocent by mistake. That's a no-brainer, that one.

My other fear? I'm afraid of people being afraid of me. Frightened people attack in self defense. Frightened people lash out. Some people really don't think the poz are human. They see monsters when they look at you, Brian, as much as when they see me. And that—that should scare you a lot more than rollover itself. That's what keeps me awake nights.

A hush falls over the set, a frozen moment where no one moves and the quiet is so deep an occasional cough can be heard over the hum of lights and other equipment.

Perky theme music begins at low volume. Brian sits up straight as it becomes louder, turns to the audience with a calm, pleased expression.

BRIAN:

Sounds like our time's up! That's another great show, everyone. Educational and entertaining, and I'm sending you home plenty to think about as always.

Thank you all, and good night!

THE END

APPENDIX 1: POWERS AND RANKINGS

Those who might develop special abilities are known poz, for positive R-factor potential. If they "roll over" from potential to active in middle age, the Department of Public Safety assigns their new abilities a letter-number-letter classification. The first letter designates their primary ability, the number gives an idea of their power level relative to others with similar abilities, and the second letter indicates any number of assorted variations or secondary characteristics.

It's a lousy system, but there are reasons for it persisting despite its flaws. An explanation can be found below this list of the power classifications currently used by the Department of Public Safety.

I. Series Designations

A: not used
This letter is reserved for the secondary variant space. It indicates a pure specimen of a particular primary power. For

example: someone classified P1A has pyrokinetic powers in the top power tier, but has no secondary powers (telekinesis or air control are common) and no physical characteristics distinguishing them from non-powered people.

B: Perceptive
This covers powers like enhanced senses, or any inexplicable abilities to sense specific traits or conditions. The variant letters for this series narrow down the nature of the perception.

C: Carnie
This slang term(considered offensive) refers to any rollover who exhibits a radical change in physical appearance. Physically deviant individuals who exhibit other powers are assigned to that series, with a variant indicator.
Individuals assigned to a primary C-series designation are basically furry, scaled, or feathered people. (See also: S-series, T series.) This Hazardous Variant tables for C's runs several hundred pages long.

D: Doctor
Individuals who can cure—or cause—disease or injury by laying on of hands or by proximity or any number of other ways laid out in the variant listings for this series. Most of the higher power-class rollovers in this series can heal *and* harm at will.

E: Projective empaths and manipulative telepaths
Not as rare as the general public believes. Sequestered on discovery and treated as deadly threats until certified safe by specialized F-series psychics.

F: Fortuneteller.
Precognition, telepathy, receptive empathy and telepathy, and clairvoyance that isn't tied to a sensory element—most of the typical psychic powers. Why F? The first psychic identified was a precog, and by then someone had already assigned P, T, and E to more obvious, common, and dangerous powers.

G: Gaia
Second-rarest series. If something is alive, or organic, or... basically if a thing exists, a G-series can affect it in some way. Most G's do not survive the rollover transformation, falling prey to the overwhelming and distorting effects of their own powers.

H: Hydro. Water elementals.

I: not used. (yet)
Too easily confused with H or lowercase L

J: Jockey.
Animal and/or plant control and/or communication.

K: Kryptonite.
A rollover whose power negates other powers. Usually specific to another power series which would be indicated by the variant letter.

L: not used yet. *See I*

M: not used. W got assigned first.

N: Nature

All natural-world related powers that don't fall into any other designation, including some air-benders and weather-workers.

O: not used. Too hard to distinguish from zero or Q.

P: Pyro
Heat and flame elementals without a concurrent earth manifestation. Various manifestations of pyrokinesis.

Q: not used.

R: Earth-movers, magma-summoners and other stone or volcanic-based powers. R was chosen because the letter falls between P for pyrokinetic and S for seismic….and S had already been by the time the first R-series power was catalogued.

S: Superhuman
Enhanced strength, speed, senses, or any combination of the three. Also used as a variant letter for carnies who are also super-strong etc.

T: *see also carnie.* Troll.
Various manifestations of skin/ height/ muscle/ weight/ strength /hormonal changes. Most have enhanced senses, all can boot their strength, speed and regeneration to enhanced levels under stress.

U & V: not used.

W: Weird.

Telekinesis and teleportation in a variety of forms from personal and passenger movement or translocation to portal opening and summoning things/people from a distance.

Y: Like A, reserved for describing variants

Z: Elevated R-factor detected, but no power develops. The rarest of primary designations, only discovered/ added after the blood tests for rollover were invented.

Additional letters — or doubled ones– are often assigned for cataloging precision, but they are rarely noted outside official paperwork. (think of the extra 4 digits in a zip code)

DPS staff with personal agendas or quotas to fill can bend definitions like pretzels to justify putting particular power manifestations into designations, and the whole set-up is vulnerable to misuse. Annual scientific conferences hold high-powered discussions about the need to revamp the whole system, but no one has come up with a better one yet.

II: Power ratings

A rating is only meaningful within a power series. There's no attempt to compare the "power" of, say, a B1 rollover who can see through foot-thick lead walls to the power of an R1 rollover who can measurably move a continent, or a W1 who can create a point-to-point teleportation gate big enough for a truck to drive through.

The number is assigned through a comprehensive set of objective tests. Results are compared to collected historical measurements, providing a consistent and impartial result.

A numeral one indicates the strongest manifestation if the

designated ability series, a rating of zero means practically no sign of the ability indicated by the primary series letter can be detected.

The change in power between rating tiers is even, but the rollover population distributes unevenly into the space.

This, like primary series designations

III: Variant designation

Every power series has an alphabet's worth of variations, far too many combinations to detail in a simple work like this. Before databases, the catalogues required multiple bindings, like an old encyclopedia set or the Reader's Guide to Periodical Literature. The early inclusion of additional letters to define powers was a white flag of cataloging surrender by the system's creators. Here are some of the complexities:

Multiple abilities are more the norm than the exception, and some power series show more variation than others.

The variants are all series dependent—the same letter means different things connected to different primaries. J stands for "jump" attached to a W teleporter, meaning altitude control, but it means a medium weight restriction when applied to a W telekinetic, and something entirely different when attached to each of the assorted B sensory powers.

Each primary variant series has its own letter/number set of deviances, and some of *those* have variances.

Series and variant assignment still relies on subjective observation and human judgment as much as hard data.

All in all this a lousy cataloging system, but its limitations stem from its origins. The people who designed it never expected it to be *permanent*. Picture the poor doctors, police, doctors, firemen and air raid wardens tasked with organizing the thousands–even tens of thousands–of hysterical, confused rollovers on that first, dreadful night in the summer of 1943. Those first responders were working in total ignorance and facing a bewildering array of symptoms. An inspired few created quick-and-dirty rules of thumb to triage their charges as quickly as possible. Accuracy and precision were not priorities.

It worked well enough to be imitated and implemented on a international scale before anyone with more sense could protest. The military and the scientific community adapted the flawed template to suit their needs and stamped it with their own flourishes, and the newborn Department of Public Safety chiseled it into the stone of bureaucracy.

It's unwieldy, and no one likes it, but unlike the Metric system (adopted by the US in 1969 and finalized in 1976 in this world) no one has come up with anything better yet. Or to be precise hundreds of excellent proposals have been offered up, but none have been effective enough to justify the upheaval and expense of changing now.

People being people, amateur cataloguers keep their eyes peeled for rare rollover types as diligently as any birdwatcher works on an Audubon life list. Trainspotters have nothing on monster buffs.

APPENDIX 2: GLOSSARY OF TERMS

A handy glossary of common slang terms and jargon.

Arsenal: a combat-trained squad of bangers

Banger: anyone with a dramatic destructive power. R's and P's in the higher power tiers, telekinetics with dramatic range or weight abilities etc.

Burnouts: slang term for early onset individuals—those who develop powers at puberty rather than middle-age. Few burnouts live past 20. Those who do are usually bangers and spend their functional years in military or law enforcement specialty units.

Carnie: a rollover with major physical manifestations. See also: geek, pistol.

Cherry bomb: female burnout

Crow: female rollover with dangerous powers

Dip: from DPS, the abbreviation for Department of Public Safety, the federal bureaucracy responsible for R-factor testing, education, and all other rollover-related issues.

Dollie: female rollover with innocuous or attractive powers

Early Onset: the official term for pubescent rollover

Flare: a power surge that accompanies a rollover exercising their abilities. Invisible to the eyes of nulls, but an auroral glow can be seen by some rollover types and appears on some visual recording media.

Joe/Little Joe: male rollover with superhuman powers but otherwise normal appearance.

Midlife Monsters: obsolete nickname for USMC Mercury Battalion

Monster Buff: fan of all things rollover-related. Many buffs keep extensive lists of rollover variant types they've ID'd "in the wild." They scour public record information for likely rare variants and share data with other buffs. Clubs meet to swap sighting information, plan sighting trips, discuss the faults of the designation system and argue over validity of each others' IDs.

Monster Marines

Null: someone with no powers/someone whose R-factor blood test is negative for rollover potential.

Pigeon: middle-aged or older female DPS employee.

Pistol: someone whose rollover power is more like a disability, likely to suicide

Poz: from R-factor positive. Someone who tests positive for the blood factor that indicates a possibility of rollover at midlife. Not a complimentary term.

Punk: a rollover with human appearance and minor powers

Pyro: pyrokinetics *and* anyone else with rollover powers that cause fires

R-factor: the blood marker that indicates a chance of developing fantastical powers. Appears in the blood at or around puberty. Mandatory testing begins at age 13.

Ranking: numerical indicator of a rollover power's strength. 1 is the highest down to 9 as the lowest, with 0 being an indicator of no measurable abilities.

Riffie: crude nickname for people who have developed midlife powers. Taken from the official designation R-Factor Active. (RFA)

Rollover: the metamorphosis that hits a small percentage of middle-aged people and invests them with super-powers and/or dramatic physical changes.

Roll cool/Roll hot: Hot rollovers develop their full active abilities in minutes or days. For the first few years after the rollover phenomenon began occurring, hot rollovers were the only kind. In recent years cool, slow rollovers have become more numerous, with a buildup to full power over weeks or months becoming the norm.

Rouster: military personnel charged with assisting the DPS in policing the powered population.

Series: official power designation. Indicated alphabetically.

Each letter indicates primary disruption type using a numerical rank scale 1-2-3-4-5-6-7-8-9-0 with 1 indicating the strongest manifestation The series and rank will usually have a sub-category letter indicating common variants that manifest with the main powers.

Slag: an insult term for particularly animalistic carnies.

Teke: Telekinetic

Torpedo: militarized water elemental or anyone with ranged water-based abilities.

Variant: letter-based system of common clusters of sub-abilities or physical variations that occur with each power.

Willie-Pete: a pyro who loses control and self-immolates.

ABOUT K. M. HERKES

K. M. HERKES writes and publishes stories that dance in the open spaces between genres. Damaged souls, triumphs of the spirit, and dialogue loaded with sarcasm are the house specialties. Professional development has included classroom teaching, animal training, aquaculture, horticulture, retail operations, and customer service. Personal development is ongoing. Cats are involved.

She lives in the Midwest and works in a library, which is exactly as exciting as it sounds. When the weather is fine she can be found in the garden more often than in the office, and at least once a year she disappears into the woods for a week to disconnect from the modern world.

Visit her website, dawnrigger.com, to find extras like story-inspired art, extended cut-scenes, excerpts, and other free fiction. You'll also find a blog of random musings and links to all the social media channels where she lurks.

Sign up for her email newsletter, and you'll receive first looks at new art and get updates on new releases.

List of Published Works

Rough Passages

Stories of the Restoration:
(in recommended reading order)
Controlled Descent
*Turning the Work**
Flight Plan
*Joining In The Round**
Novices

*collected together in paperback as *Weaving In the Ends*

Made in the USA
Las Vegas, NV
29 August 2022

54326029R00125